MINERVA CRIES
MURDER

Also by Mignon F. Ballard

Raven Rock
Cry at Dusk
Deadly Promise
The Widow's Woods
Final Curtain

For Young Readers

Aunt Matilda's Ghost

MINERVA CRIES MURDER

An Eliza Figg Mystery

Mignon F. Ballard

Carroll & Graf Publishers, Inc.
New York

M
Ballard

First Carroll & Graf edition 1993

Carroll & Graf Publishers, Inc.
260 Fifth Avenue
New York, NY 10001

Library of Congress Cataloging-in-Publication Data

Ballard, Mignon Franklin.
    Minerva cries murder : an Eliza Figg mystery / Mignon F.
Ballard.
        p.   cm.
    ISBN 0-88184-946-4 : $18.95
    I. Title.
    PS3552.A466M56   1993
    813'.54—dc20   92-38239
                                                              CIP

Manufactured in the United States of America

This book is dedicated with affection
to my teachers and classmates at Calhoun Schools
who endured my constant scribbling.

MINERVA CRIES
MURDER

CHAPTER ONE

The hound of hell was loose again. Eliza heard his frenzied barking over the monotonous pounding of January rain. It was late afternoon, almost dark, and outside her window a tall pine creaked in the wind as its branches slapped the eaves. Somewhere a window rattled. The whole place was falling apart. Once-white paint peeled in dingy curls, and a damp blob blossomed on the dining room ceiling. It would take more than paint to hold 410 North Habersham together, but Eliza didn't plan to stay long, so why bother?

The dog's barking grew louder, more menacing, and Eliza jumped as a log fell apart in the fireplace sending orange sparks up the chimney. The Thornbroughs were going to have to do something about that awful dog. The Boss, they called him. The Beast would have been more appropriate. The German shepherd mix terrified joggers and neighborhood children alike, and had snacked objectively on representatives from the Jehovah's Witnesses, two youthful Mormon missionaries, and the finance committee from Minerva United Methodist Church. The post office no longer delivered there.

Somebody yelled—it sounded like a woman's voice. Hurried footsteps thudded on the front porch, and whoever was there held a finger on the doorbell while knocking frantically on the leaded glass panels.

"Hold on, I'm coming!" Eliza stumbled to her feet, losing one shoe under the sofa in the process. No time to fish it out now. The person seeking refuge at the door was going to crash through the window if The Boss didn't devour her first. Eliza found herself wondering where you would go to replace glass that had been installed in 1915.

Behind the dreary rain-soaked figure, Eliza saw the snarling dog bound across her yard and skid through the puddled walk. Quickly she wrenched open the door. "Hurry! Hurry! Come inside . . . the door wasn't locked."

A young woman in a soggy brown coat hurled herself upon her and shivered between great sobbing gulps as Eliza slammed the door. The dog made a couple of obligatory lunges and wandered off in search of fresh blood.

"God, that was close!" The dripping stranger crouched in the hallway as if hugging herself for warmth. "Oh, hell!" she said. "I think I've just wet my pants."

Painfully pregnant. Those were the words that came to mind. The woman was thin and pale. Her drab hair hung about her face like frazzled yarn, and her enormous stomach strained against the confines of her coat. She couldn't be much older than nineteen and she looked about ten months along. The baby had consumed her.

"It's the rain. You're drenched, and it's cold here in the hall. Come and get warm by the fire. Let me get you something hot to drink." Eliza tried to take her arm but the girl shied away.

"If I could just change, get into something dry, I'll be okay. I'm sorry; I didn't mean to be so much trouble." The woman shivered as water—and whatever else— dripped onto the rose-flowered scatter rug Eliza's Grandmother Adelaide had brought from Macon in 1937. And for the first time Eliza noticed the green canvas bag at her feet.

"I don't suppose . . . would it be okay if I cleaned up somewhere? I could really use a bath." The poor thing seemed worse than miserable. Wet hair dripped onto her collar, and her shoes looked as if they might squish. What harm could it do?

"There's a bathroom at the end of the hall. Take your time, have a good, long soak." Eliza turned to show her the way, lay out clean towels, but the woman moved ahead, the bulging overnight bag bumped her thin legs as she walked. She seemed to know where she was going.

"Here, let me take that." Eliza took the bag and pulled a towel from the bathroom shelf—a thick plum-colored towel that smelled of her mother's lavender sachet. She bent over the huge claw-footed tub and watched steaming water cover the scrubbed white porcelain. "Better get off those wet clothes before you catch cold. Hurry now! Are you all right? Is there anything else you need?" Eliza almost bit her tongue. She sounded just like her mother.

The strange young woman had removed her coat and folded it over the sink, and her wet sneakers stood side by side oozing onto the faded green bath mat. Soggy pink socks lay in a wad in the corner.

She's waiting for you to leave, stupid, Eliza reminded herself. She's modest—and who wouldn't be with a belly the size of the Capitol dome!

"Is there someone you'd like me to call?" Eliza asked, rising to her feet. Surely this very pregnant young woman had a reason for walking past her house on a cold, wet January evening. A concerned husband must be combing the streets, a prospective grandfather pacing the floor, but the girl didn't answer. Maybe she hadn't heard.

Impulsively, Eliza tossed a bath cube into the swirling water and the scent of honeysuckle wafted up to meet her. She checked the water temperature and dried her hand on her shirt. "By the way, I'm Eliza Figg."

"I know." The woman smiled, and for a minute Eliza thought she was going to cry again. "I'm Melody. Melody Lamb. You probably don't remember me. I was a little girl when I stayed here, about five or six I guess."

Melody Lamb pulled a pink ribbon from her dripping ponytail and began to unbutton her smock. "Your mother, Miss Martha, she was the sweetest thing—so good to me . . ."

"Melody?" Eliza looked closer at the thin triangular face, clear hazel eyes. Could this be the little waif who had lived with her family for part of a year, followed her everywhere, made her read *Snow White* so many times she knew it by heart?

Melody sat on the edge of the tub and trailed her hand in the water. "Miss Martha—she's not—"

"My mother died last summer." Eliza turned to shut off the faucets. Her words sounded hard, final.

"Mama talked about you a lot," Eliza said, softening. "We often wondered where you were, what became of you."

Melody almost smiled. "Well, now you know." She dug a small bottle of sample shampoo from her bag and set it on the shelf above the tub. "I thought you'd be off riding camels or something. Last time I talked with somebody from here, they said you'd joined the Peace Corps. You always did like to do neat stuff like that—didn't expect to find you still in Minerva."

"Neither did I," Eliza said. "That was a few years ago."

"What about your dad? Big Ben, I used to call him. He said they named that clock after him."

"Big Ben's gone a little cuckoo," Eliza said, gathering the woman's cast-off clothing. "He's chiming 'The Wedding March' now . . . married a widow from Atlanta two weeks ago and went off on one of those luxury cruises. Mama's only been gone six months, and here he is making a great big fool of himself over a woman at least fifteen years younger!"

Melody's eyes widened. "Oh," she said, looking away.

"Thinks he has money, I guess. Or maybe he thinks she does. I reckon they deserve each other!" She slammed the door on the way out.

Eliza found a box of instant hot chocolate on the top shelf in the kitchen and turned on the burner under the kettle. Melody looked as if she could do with something warm inside her. Come to think of it, she probably was hungry too. Weren't mothers-to-be supposed to be always starving?

She heated a can of vegetable beef soup—that should have plenty of vitamins in it—and sliced the rest of the Christmas ham her neighbor Dorcas Youngblood had brought over. Since she had come home to Minerva the spring before to care for her dying mother, and then her grieving father, the people in the little Georgia town had made a point of looking after her—without seeming obvious, of course.

"I made a big pot of soup today, Eliza, thought you might like some" . . . "They're offering two pizzas for the price of one, why don't you join us" . . . "We're having oyster stew on Christmas Eve, and I know how much you like it . . ." Eliza thanked the Lord the holidays were behind her and that the local drugstore had a sale on Drink-Thin in four delicious flavors. She had stocked up on Chocolate Sin.

She heard the water drain from the tub and turned the soup on low. Melody hadn't mentioned a husband, hadn't seemed concerned about letting anyone know where she was. What was she doing here? Was she a single mother looking for a place to have her baby? She looked as if she might deliver at any time.

Eliza filled two holly-trimmed mugs with cocoa mix, spilling brown powder on the blue speckled countertop. Did Melody Lamb plan to stay *here?* With *her?* What would she do if the woman went into labor?

Although the expectant mother had the clear, alabaster skin and delicate features of someone in her late teens, Eliza knew she was at least twenty-one. It had been about sixteen years since the little girl had come to stay with the Figgs until their neighbor who worked in social services could place her with a family. Eliza had been twelve.

The child had been abandoned as a toddler, and the couple who planned to adopt her backed out only a few weeks before Christmas.

Kindhearted Martha Figg took Melody into her home as a favor to her friend, but when the child was adopted eight months later, she cried as if she were giving up her own.

And now she was back. Apparently alone. Eliza rapped on the bathroom door and offered her a thick terry robe. "Don't bother getting dressed," she said. "It's late, and you must be tired. I've heated up a little supper, why don't you just plan to stay the night?"

Melody claimed the robe with a skinny white arm and a smiling face. "Do you mean it? Oh, that would be wonderful! Do you think I might sleep in my old room?"

The relief in her voice was so obvious, Eliza didn't trust herself to answer.

Later, as she washed the few supper dishes, Eliza noticed the young woman staring out the sitting-room window as if she were looking for someone, someone she didn't want to see. Like a sentinel she stood to one side and lifted the curtain to peer into the street.

Eliza frowned. Was Melody afraid to be seen, or afraid of what she might see? Maybe she was still frightened of The Boss.

"The dog won't come back," she said from the kitchen doorway. "I phoned the Thornbroughs and they've promised to lock him up. This time I've threatened to call the dogcatcher, and they know good and well I mean it. I don't think we'll have to worry about him again."

But although her guest seemed mildly relieved at this news, Eliza noticed she continued to glance out at the dark winter night.

"Melody, are you expecting someone? Is anything wrong?" Eliza threw the dish towel over the back of the sofa and gave the dying fire a poke. "Come and sit down, tell me about yourself. We have a lot of catching up to do." *Like, are you married, and if so where the hell is your husband?*

But her guest wasn't in a mood to confide. "I'm just kind of restless, I guess. It's getting pretty close to my time, you know."

"Like how close?" Don't do this to me, God, Eliza thought.

"Not for another week at least, don't worry." Melody smiled. It was a tired smile, just about the tiredest smile Eliza had ever seen on anyone that young. "I'm getting kind of sleepy," she said. "Do you mind if we talk tomorrow?"

"Of course not." Eliza found herself apologizing. How very thoughtless of her! What did a few hours matter? But for a long time after her visitor had gone up to bed, she still puzzled over the woman's reappearance. In spite of what Melody had said, she seemed afraid of something. And she looked so helpless—at odds with herself. Surely she had a home somewhere. A family.

Well, it wasn't her concern, Eliza thought, yawning. As soon as she could work things out to get back to graduate school, she would quit her temporary job at historic Bellawood, and put Minerva, Georgia, behind her for good. She switched off the hall light and went up to bed. Tomorrow she would find out what this was all about. Tomorrow Miss (Mrs.? Ms.?) Melody Lamb was going right back where she belonged.

CHAPTER TWO

Was she going to sleep forever? Eliza stood in the hallway listening for sounds of movement behind the closed door. It was after ten, yet the room where Melody Lamb slept was as silent as a—

No, not that! People didn't die having babies anymore. Did they? Eliza quietly opened the door and looked inside. Melody lay on her back, (how else?) her chest rising and falling in easy rhythm. Eliza looked down at her, feeling oddly maternal. Except for her swollen abdomen, she looked almost childlike sleeping there in the same maple bed she had slept in as a five year old.

Martha Figg had repapered the room when her granddaughter, Sally, was born. Eliza's sister's child was now ten and lived in Virginia, but gray and yellow kittens still chased butterflies around a flowered border. Somehow it suited the present tenant, Eliza thought.

She tiptoed out and closed the door softly behind her, glad it was Sunday and she wouldn't have to go to work. Downstairs in the kitchen Eliza thumbed through her mother's recipes. Maybe a hearty breakfast would loosen Melody's tongue, and she knew her grandmother's hand-written recipe for buttermilk waffles was in that file some-where. Of course there was her sworn intention to diet, but Eliza couldn't remember the last time she'd had but-termilk waffles—so crispy on the outside and light as a lullaby inside. And they were even better with sausages. Now, where did her mother keep that old waffle iron?

She didn't have any buttermilk, but Dorcas Young-blood did. Of course borrowing from her next door neighbor meant explaining why she was going to the trouble of making waffles from scratch, which meant tell-ing her about Melody's return. Dorcas Youngblood was her mother's closest friend and had lived next door since Eliza was a baby. What Dorcas didn't know hadn't yet happened.

"You mean that tiny little girl with those great big eyes is pregnant? Why, I can't believe it! She wasn't any bigger than an elf." Dorcas looked almost threatening as she sloshed buttermilk into a cup.

Eliza reminded her that sixteen years had elapsed since Melody wore fringed bangs and played topless in the sprinkler.

"Then where's her husband?" Dorcas closed the refrig-erator door with a heave of her ample hips.

"Don't know; that's what I plan to find out."

"But there must be something! Aren't you going to—"

Eliza paused at the back door, cup in hand. "When *I* know, *you'll* know. I promise."

"You mean you've made me late for church for that?" Dorcas snatched her purse and car keys from the table and followed her outside. "Believe you me," she said over the slamming of the door, "something's rotten in Sweden! And by the way, those waffles freeze real good if you seal'em up tight."

"That's Denmark," Eliza said, laughing. "And thanks, I'll remember that."

She heard footsteps overhead when she got back home

and hurried to stir up the batter for breakfast. She would feed her guest first and then ask questions. Eliza wondered if Melody's adopted parents knew where she was. It took her a few minutes to think of their name: Sutherland. Lived somewhere on the other side of Atlanta at the time. Nearing middle age, the couple was willing to take an older child, but the little girl had cried when she left the Figgs.

Eliza remembered the Sutherlands bringing Melody for visits a few times that first year or so. By then the child seemed happy enough with the couple, and they obviously adored her. "Look, 'Liza, I get to dress like Sunday every day," Melody had said, showing off her lace-trimmed socks and shiny black patent leather shoes. Melody had loved pretty clothes better than anything, and it was hard to believe that this was the same young woman who yesterday had seemed resigned to faded maternity jeans and a shapeless smock.

But at least her appetite was still good. The mother-to-be put away two and a half waffles, three sausage patties, and half a pitcher of blackberry syrup, then washed it all down with an iced-tea glass full of orange juice. If Eliza hadn't fed her supper the night before, she would have sworn Melody was on the verge of starvation.

"I just can't seem to get enough citrus fruit," Melody said, gulping the last few swallows. "Must be a craving or something."

Now. Eliza shoved aside her plate and crossed her arms in front of her. "Who's your doctor, Melody?"

She licked syrup off a finger. "Dr. Curtis back in Stone Mountain; at least he was—still is, I guess. I haven't seen him lately."

"What do you mean you haven't seen him lately? Aren't your visits supposed to be closer together about now?"

Melody twisted her paper napkin into a frilly bow and stared into her lap—or what was left of it. "I don't want to go back home." She spoke softly, so softly Eliza had to lean forward to hear.

"Why not? Melody, where is this baby's father? Does he know where you are?" Did the jerk not even care?

"He's gone."

"Gone? Gone where? Is he coming back?"

"He can't come back. He's dead. Drowned."

Eliza felt herself sinking, smothering in a pile of dirty diapers, sour-smelling bibs, and those disgusting strained things babies ate. She hadn't been exactly thrilled when her parents had taken Melody to their hearts all those years ago. Her only sibling, Katherine, had been away at college, and Eliza had discovered that being an only child wasn't all that bad.

Now her mother had up and died on her; her father was off floating around on the Love Boat somewhere, and guess who had to deal with little Melody?

You cold, unfeeling clod, said a Goodie-Two-Shoes voice inside her. *This poor young thing is alone and pregnant. And crying. Can't you see she's crying?*

Eliza emptied the juice container into Melody's glass and offered a fresh supply of paper napkins. "I'm sorry, Melody. Tell me, what happened? And when?"

"The weekend after Thanksgiving . . . remember how warm it was? Like summer almost, and Sonny had gone fishing up on Lake Lanier." Melody pressed a napkin against one eye, and then the other.

"By himself?"

"Uh-huh. Said it was probably the last chance he'd have before the baby came. And it was." Melody grabbed another napkin to stem the fresh flow. "Sonny just loved fishing. I was going to give him a new tackle box for Christmas . . ."

"Sonny was—your husband?"

"Of course." Melody looked offended. "We'd only been married a year and a half. Sonny wanted to finish college first. We met at Georgia State, you know."

Eliza didn't know. She didn't know a lot of things. "Do they know how it happened?" she asked.

Melody shook her head. "Looked like his boat flipped over. Must've hit his head. Sonny was a good swimmer; I guess that's why he wasn't wearing a life vest."

Eliza poured herself another cup of coffee. Melody declined. It made her feel yucky, she said. "What about your parents," Eliza asked. "The Sutherlands. Do they know where you are?"

"Dad died when I was in high school, and Mom's in a nursing home in Marietta. Been there two years. Alzheimers." Melody shrugged. "Most days she doesn't even know I'm there."

Eliza looked away. At least her own mother had been alert until the end, except for those last few days when she'd lapsed into a coma. Cheated cancer of the pain, her father said. Eliza hoped it was true.

"Look, I don't want you to think I'm begging or anything." Melody looked across the table with those huge eyes deep enough to tread water in. "Sonny left me money; his job didn't pay all that much, but the insurance will take care of us for a while. I'm not starving."

Oh Lord! Could the woman read her mind? "I didn't mean to give you that impression," Eliza told her. "It's just that you seemed . . . well, nervous. You said you didn't want to go home. Is it because you dread being alone? What about friends? Neighbors?"

"We've only been in this apartment since September," Melody said. "And I was working up until Sonny—well, until this happened. We didn't get to know many neighbors."

"What about people at work?"

Melody poked at a piece of waffle with her fork, making a trail through the sticky syrup. "They're friendly enough and all, and they were real nice to me after Sonny died, but there's nobody special—you know, like a good friend. I just started working there back in the summer. It was a temporary job."

Melody sighed. "We kept meaning to join a church, but we never did."

Eliza stood and put the dishes in the sink. Everything about this woman-child seemed to be temporary—except her baby. Babies came to stay. But not here, Eliza thought. Dear Lord, please, not here!

"Your mama—she was so good to me, always made me feel special, you know." Melody heaved herself up and added her dirty glass to the stack in the sink. "I was hoping she'd be here. Miss Martha could tell me what to do."

Eliza nodded. That goes for both of us, she thought, dumping entirely too much detergent into the foaming water.

Melody paused to look out the window, craning to see the street. Absently she picked up the blue ceramic pitcher and poured the remaining syrup back into the bottle.

Eliza tried not to make a face as Melody put the syrup bottle in the wrong place in the cabinet without even wiping it off. Just leave it be, she thought. It doesn't matter. Melody Lamb was alone and desperate. The man she loved had been suddenly taken from her just as she was about to become a mother. And she had to be as uncomfortable as the fat lady's horse. But that didn't explain why the woman kept looking over her shoulder.

Eliza watched her walk into the living room and take her station by the window. There she goes, hanging onto those curtains again. "Melody Lamb," Eliza said. "What in the world are you looking for out there?"

CHAPTER THREE

"What do you mean?" Melody let the curtain drop.

"If you had a musket, you could guard the fort," Eliza said. "Why do you keep looking out the window? Is somebody coming?"

"I'm not—"

"Look, Melody, unless something spectacular has sprouted overnight, there's nothing out in that street that's worth all this attention. Something's wrong. What is it?"

"You'll think I'm losing it . . ." Melody picked up a magazine and flipped through it. It was Ben Figg's January copy of *Golf Digest*, Eliza noticed, but he didn't need it now. He had other interests. Melody tossed it aside. "Somebody's following me," she said.

"Who? What makes you think that?"

"I don't know. I just feel it—I know it." Melody shuddered. "Gives me the creeps."

"Have you actually seen somebody?"

"Well, not really, not up close. But there's a car, a black car; a big one. Cadillac, I think, or maybe a Lin-

coln. I've seen it parked across the street from our apartment, and once or twice I noticed it in the parking lot
where I worked."

"When was this?"

"Oh, way back in the fall. I first saw it sometime in
October, then I didn't see it for a while. But a few weeks
ago it showed up again. And once when I was walking
back from the drugstore, I knew there was somebody behind me, but every time I turned around he slowed down.
I never got a look at his face."

"But you know it was a man?" Eliza watched her eyes.
Sometimes you could tell when people weren't telling the
truth, but Melody's fear seemed genuine.

Melody nodded, clutching Martha Figg's needlepoint
sofa pillow to her chest. "Well, I think it was a man, but
he was too far away to be sure."

"A lot of people drive big black cars, Melody," Eliza
said. "It might have belonged to somebody in your apartment building who works where you do. And other people use the sidewalks too. What makes you think he was
following you?"

"I told you you'd think I was crazy!" Melody threw the
pillow aside. "It happens a lot now—that feeling, especially when I'm in crowded places. I've gotten to where I
just hate to go to the store. So many people! I feel like I
meet myself around every corner . . . and sometimes,
well . . . I see things."

"What kind of things?"

"I don't know. Things that ought not be there." She
shrugged. "Imagination, I guess."

"Would anybody have a reason to follow you?"

Melody shook her head. "Not that I know of."

"What about Sonny? Is there anything in his background? Something he might not have told you?"

"I can't imagine," Melody said. "He came from a big
family up in Tennessee. He was the baby, and the first to
leave home. They all came down here to our wedding—

nice people, but they never had much. Sonny put himself through school, you know."

Melody looked as if she might cry again and Eliza didn't know what to do. She knew what her mother would do. Martha Figg would hold her, comfort her, and somehow she would make everything seem brighter. Eliza wished she were here.

Sitting beside her, Eliza took Melody's small hand. It was cold. "What's happening to you sounds like a phobia," she said. "Agoraphobia, I think it's called. It's a fear of being in public places. A lot of people have it." She lied. Eliza didn't know of any who did, but she'd heard of a few.

"Or it could be some kind of panic attack. After all the trauma you've been through lately, it's a wonder you're not an emotional blob," Eliza said. "That's another reason to see your doctor, Melody. He can tell you what to do."

"But it started before that happened." Melody gripped Eliza's fingers so hard she had to pull away. "Everything was fine, really."

"I guess expectant mothers have different reactions to what's going on inside them," Eliza said. She remembered how her friend Sydney had a thing about riding in cars when she was pregnant. And her sister had been afraid of dogs.

Melody smiled when she told her this, reminding Eliza of how she had looked at five. "So you think it—this phobia or whatever—will go away?"

"Probably, yes, but I'm not a doctor. You need to see your doctor . . . what's his name? Curtis. He'll know more about it than I do."

"Aren't there doctors here?"

"Well, sure—but they don't have your records, your medical history. It's a little late to change obstetricians now."

"But I want to have my baby here—in Minerva. I feel safer here."

Eliza recognized the tone. *But I want to hear* Snow White *again . . . But I don't like green beans . . . But Miss Martha said I don't have to go to bed . . .*

"Well, you can't!" Eliza didn't mean to speak so sharply, but she had had enough upheaval in her life. What was this person trying to do to her? "Look, Melody, I can't take care of you—much less a baby. I have a job; besides, I don't plan to stay here long myself."

She had come back only because of her mother. Then her father—always the solid, dependable one who could be counted on to make her smile, had withdrawn into himself with despair. Eliza had given up her teaching assistantship at Warrenton University and put her Ph.D. on hold. In June her professor was offered a better position at a university in California and invited Eliza to come along and finish there. She couldn't leave her parents, then, of course. And later, after her mother died, she told herself, it would be cruel to move so far away from this stranger of a father who seldom spoke or smiled.

At the same time trustees of the restored plantation, Bellawood, birthplace of Pentecost Pitts, one of the state's earlier governors and Minerva's only prominent native son, were looking for someone to help entice visitors to Echota County and to their forty-two acres of Georgia history. Eliza accepted the job on the condition that they find someone to replace her by the end of the year. They hadn't, of course, and Eliza hadn't insisted. The subject of her dissertation: *Social and Political Upheaval in Rural Areas of the South in the Years Following the War Between the States* seemed remote and unchallenging. Maybe it was because she'd been away too long.

Reluctantly, Eliza began to renew old acquaintances from high school days, and had even gone out a few times with Baxter Phillips whose construction company was currently renovating the Pitts family chapel at Bellawood.

*   *   *

Working hours at Bellawood were sometimes sporadic, and if the woman who was to teach a quilting class hadn't gotten sick and cancelled, Eliza would have been there when Melody came seeking refuge, she reminded herself. And she winced at the thought of Melody's terrified face as The Boss lunged after her.

"You're not being practical," Eliza said, trying to make Melody meet her eyes. "Why, you didn't even bring any clothes, except for what's in that overnight bag—not to mention things for the baby." Did she think they came with a complete wardrobe?

Melody sat staring at her hands which were clasped tightly in her lap, as if she were praying. She looked absolutely miserable. "I know," she said quietly. "They're at the bus station."

"Where?"

"The bus station. I came on the bus because I was afraid to drive here by myself. My luggage is in a locker there along with some stuff for the baby. My car and most of my other things are back at the apartment though."

"You mean in Stone Mountain?"

Melody nodded, not looking up.

Nice planning, Eliza thought. "And had you already decided where you were going to stay?"

Melody smiled. "Well, I hoped to stay here. The phone is still listed in your dad's name, so I thought Miss Martha might put me up. I was almost here when that awful dog started after me!"

Eliza suddenly remembered she hadn't even thought to bring in the Sunday paper and decided that this would be a good time to do it. If she sat here another minute she might say something . . . Well, she just might say something.

The Atlanta Constitution lay in its usual resting place in the roots of the big red oak her great-grandfather had planted when he built the house. The tree took up most of one side of the front yard and its shade kept the downstairs bedroom excessively dark, but since her father had

married and moved with his Olivia to Atlanta, nobody
slept there anyway. Besides, as Martha Figg had often
pointed out, in the summer you could sit on the front
porch, concealed by the foliage, and observe their section of Habersham Street without being seen.

Now the neighborhood was almost deserted except for
Jessie Gilreath plowing into her driveway a few houses
down the street; coming home from church no doubt. It
was about that time. Eliza could see Jessie's orange hair
from where she stood. "Hot turd" orange, her friend Sydney called it. "Looks just like a fresh dropped cow patty
—you can almost see the steam rise from it," Syd insisted.

Eliza found herself standing out in the cold front yard
smiling to herself as she watched her neighbor retrieve
her newspaper from the thorny pyracantha by the walk
and march rigidly inside. The local distributor of *The
Constitution* would hear about this, Eliza thought. Jessie
Gilreath loved to show off the collection of perfect-atten-
dance pins she had earned for never missing a day of
Sunday school in twenty-seven years at Mount Zion Baptist Church, but forgiveness wasn't one of her priorities.
She never had forgotten that Martha Figg had taken first
prize at the Minerva May-Fest Garden Show three years
in a row. That was almost twenty years ago.

Eliza glanced over her shoulder at the empty street half
expecting to see a threatening black car loom on the hori-
zon. Of course none did. She couldn't tell if Melody was
lying, or simply exaggerating. But she was here. Now.
And she was pregnant. This baby wasn't going to wait.

"All right." Eliza stood facing Melody across the room.
It was a little past high noon, but it was a duel just the
same. "You can stay here for a few days—just until we
find you another place. It will have to be a furnished
apartment, at least until after the baby comes. You're in
no condition to move right now." She frowned. "Look,
I'm sort of in limbo until I can get back in school and pick

up where I left off with this degree. I don't even know how long I'll be here myself. I'm sorry, Melody, I just can't ask you to live here. You do understand, don't you?''

Melody nodded mutely, but Eliza thought she saw the spark of victory in her eyes.

Chapter Four

"You want me to drive you where?" Even over the telephone, Sydney's voice jumped at Eliza with a drill sergeant's bark. The mother of four untamed children —all under eight—including five-year-old twins, Syd McClanahan sometimes had to be reminded that not everyone was about to bathe the cat in the toilet or feed the baby out of the dog's dish.

Eliza only smiled. She was used to it. "Stone Mountain," she said. "I have to pick up a car—plus a few other things. Tell you about it on the way."

"But that's over an hour's drive! Jonathan would never sit still for that."

Eliza agreed. Syd's squirming three year old would have to stop at every bathroom along the way. "Couldn't Eddie's mother keep him?"

Pause. "Well, I was kind of saving her for the Valentine dance, but she'd have to pick up the other three anyway. What about work? Aren't you supposed to be at Bellawood tomorrow?"

"One of the docents is filling in, besides, they owe me one after that Christmas open house. Made so many cotton boll wreathes my fingers bled."

"Oh, quit yer belly achin'! You pulled in a profit, didn't you?"

Syd thought it over. "Well, all right, if I can con Eddie's mom, but you owe me one."

"Right. I'll drive your Aunt Clarise to the doctor, walk your dog, make a birthday cake for the next celebration . . . you name it—"

"Babysit for the Valentine dance?" Sydney laughed her throaty chuckle.

". . . Paint and paper your entire house, mow your lawn for a year, send your oldest to college . . ." Eliza paused for breath.

"Just kidding! When should I come by for you?"

Melody was still asleep when Eliza left the next morning. As she climbed in the station wagon beside her friend, Eliza thought of the time they had cut school together and spent the whole day in Atlanta with her father's gasoline credit card and less than ten dollars between them. They had a wonderful time and came home with thirty cents to spare, but they had paid for it. Three days suspension, no phone for weeks, and a two thousand word paper on their principal's favorite subject: *Becoming a Responsible Adult.*

Syd must have been thinking the same thing. "I have three dollars and eighty-six cents. How much do you have?"

Eliza grinned. "A big, fat five dollar bill and two quarters. Let's go!"

Syd laughed. "It was worth it, wasn't it? Would you do it again?"

"In a minute. Is Singing Sol still principal?"

"Either that or his mummy is walking the halls—still humming off-key. I was over there for the Blood Mobile last fall, and he came up and shook my hand, then couldn't think of my name."

"Maybe it's just as well," Eliza told her. She was glad of her seat belt as Syd veered onto the ramp to I-85, then darted into the fast-moving traffic. Since high school Sydney had accumulated a college degree, a husband, four children, about fifteen extra pounds, and an assortment of domestic talents previously unsuspected, but she still drove like an eighteen year old.

Now she frowned at Eliza as she sped past a slow-moving truck. "Well, are you going to tell me or not? Why am I driving you to Stone Mountain on a dreary January Monday when I have about sixteen loads of dirty laundry and a kitchen floor that's trapping flies?"

Eliza told her.

"Oh, Lord," Syd said. "Oh, Lord."

"What? *What?*"

"Sounds to me like you're stuck, *Aunt* Eliza. Hope you know Lamaze."

"You mean that breathing exercise where they have babies with no anesthetic? No way!"

Syd just grinned. "Say good-bye to your lifestyle as you now know it, Eliza Figg. No more impromptu skiing trips to Sugar Mountain or white-water rafting on the Chattooga—and backpacking in the Himalayas is definitely out."

"That was during my Peace Corps days," Eliza reminded her. *"One time* I backpacked in the Himalayas. Give me a break, Syd. Besides, I'm not changing my lifestyle. Not going to be here that long."

"What are you going to do, put her out on the street?"

"Of course not! But I thought a furnished apartment . . . doesn't Eleanor Jackson rent out the back of her house?" Eleanor loved babies.

"Her mother's living there now," Sydney said. "But there must be some place. I'll ask around."

Eliza drew in her breath. "Hurry," she said.

Earlier that day she had spoken with the receptionist at the local obstetrics clinic and made an appointment for Melody the next day. She had also given them the name of Melody's doctor in Stone Mountain so they could transfer her records. The woman Eliza spoke with had been reluctant to accept Melody as a patient so close to her delivery date until Eliza explained the circumstances. But after all, what choice did they have? What choice did she have?

"Tell me I'm not a rotten person," Eliza said as they neared the outskirts of Atlanta.

"Okay. You're not a rotten person. Who said you were?"

"My conscience." Eliza heard herself groan. "Every time I look at Melody Lamb I want to shake her for doing this to me. Here she is, alone in the world with all these changes going on in her life, and the one person she turns to acts like a selfish jerk. But I can't help it. I resent the hell out of her!"

Sydney shrugged. "Who wouldn't?" She laughed. "Sounds like 'Same song, second verse . . .' "

" 'Could get better, but it's gonna get worse.' " Eliza finished the quote. "Thanks a bunch."

"I was just thinking about the day she came the first time, remember? It was right before Christmas, and your mother shamed you into giving her your doll—the pretty one you kept on your window seat. The one in the yellow dress."

"With a straw bonnet. Victoria Antoinette. She had long black hair, these tiny little flowers on her slippers, and a green parasol that opened and shut. She was the prettiest doll I ever had—and the last one. I didn't want to give her away."

"Serves you right for naming her Victoria Antoinette," Syd said. "It's enough to gag a maggot, Eliza! I'd forgotten you had such disgusting taste."

"For heaven's sake, I was only ten when I got her!"

Eliza had never played with Victoria Antoinette, except to brush her long hair or wash and iron the doll's lace-trimmed organdy. And for several years Victoria Antoinette had sat enthroned in Eliza's bedroom window with her stuffed bear, Mr. Grundy, and a bedraggled Raggedy Ann. Until Melody came.

"It's funny you should mention that doll," Eliza said. "I said something about her to Melody last night—wondered whatever became of her. She didn't remember the doll's name or the yellow dress or anything."

"She was only five or six," Syd reminded her. "Besides, she probably gave her another name—if she had any aesthetic judgment at all."

Eliza grinned and stuck out her tongue. Melody probably had a roomful of dolls after she went to live with the Sutherlands, but how could anyone forget those dainty flowered slippers and the green parasol?

"Melody thinks she's being followed," Eliza said.

"Really? Why?"

"She doesn't know, only that it's somebody in a big black car. She's always watching out the window. Scared of her shadow. And last night she woke up crying—said somebody was trying to smother her. Is that normal, Syd?"

"You're asking *me* what's normal? I wouldn't worry about it though, at least not until after the baby comes."

But as they drew closer to Stone Mountain, Eliza almost expected to see a huge black vehicle waiting by Melody's apartment building. Thank goodness none fit the description!

It took the rest of the morning and numerous trips up and down stairs to pack the items Melody would need into the back of her aging blue Honda. The stroller and bassinet, although sturdy, looked as if they had been bought at yard sales, but the playpen and infant car seat seemed new.

Eliza thought of the young couple shopping, planning

for their baby, and how proud they must have been of their purchases.

"What's the matter?" Sydney asked. "Something wrong?"

"Back aches a little, that's all." Eliza hid behind a large box of diapers.

By the time they wedged in the baby furniture, plus a few other things Melody had requested, Eliza barely had room for herself behind the wheel. She was surprised to find that the one thing Melody had seemed most eager for was a bulky box of books. Cookbooks. So far her guest had shown no interest in helping with meals, but at her stage, who could blame her?

"Is this all?" Syd asked as they stood in the small living room with the last items—a bundle of soiled laundry and a meager stack of towels.

"Except for some of her mother's things that she keeps in storage," Eliza said. The room looked bleak with its faded slipcovers and beige carpeting, although Melody had obviously attempted to brighten the apartment with flowered print draperies framing the window facing the parking lot. The only personal belongings seemed to be a watercolor of purple iris and a pot of English ivy on the coffee table.

"I'll get them," Syd said, following Eliza's gaze, and she crossed the room to lift the picture from the wall.

Eliza waited by the door. "Let's stop for lunch somewhere. I'm starving. My treat."

But Syd stood by the window looking out at the parking lot below. Silently she waved her arm, beckoning Eliza to join her.

"Remember that big black car you told me about? Well, there's one; see it? In the corner of the lot there. Waiting."

Eliza laughed, or tried to. "Come on, you'll have me as paranoid as Melody." She frowned. "But let's find out; we'll give him a test. Remember that barbecue place near Kennesaw?"

Sydney nodded. "The Three Pigs—but will they re-member me? The last time I stopped there they offered all you can eat for $7.95, and I thought they were going to ask me to leave."

"Maybe they won't recognize you," Eliza said as they walked outside together. "Is that car still there? Can you get a look at the license plate?"

"Not without being obvious. If they're really looking for Melody, whoever it is has surely noticed us coming in and out of her apartment. Why don't you go first, and I'll try to pull in behind them, then meet you at the restau-rant?"

Eliza agreed. The Three Pigs was about thirty-five miles away on a lesser traveled side road. If the black car turned up there—well, maybe Melody wasn't so para-noid after all.

Since the restaurant was a popular place to eat, Eliza wasn't surprised to find the parking lot almost full. She found a space at the far end and was relieved to see Sydney pull in a few minutes later. She had only had time for toast and juice at breakfast, and could almost taste the barbecue.

"Well," Eliza said, inhaling the hickory smoke as she met her by the entrance. "Did you see him? Did he fol-low me?"

Sydney shrugged. "Not that I could tell. I waited a few minutes to give him a chance. Of course he could've been behind me."

Eliza shook her head. "Let's face it—I think Melody's just plain neurotic. Not to say she doesn't have good rea-sons; I just hope it doesn't last." Her stomach rumbled noisily. "Come on, let's get a table. Something tells me I'm going to need the nourishment."

But Sydney, usually the first one in the chow line, hung back. "What's the matter?" Eliza paused. "Why are you staring?"

Sydney shaded her eyes and frowned. "That car that

just went past . . . does that look like the same one to
you?"

The car was big and black and seemed to be in a hurry.
Eliza squinted, then shrugged. "For all I know it could
have been a hearse. Whatever it is, it's gone now. Let's
eat!"

CHAPTER FIVE

ella Pitts, mother of Pentecost, looked disapprovingly at Eliza from her portrait over the mantel at Bellawood. Her dark hair, parted in the middle, was pulled back so tightly it made her ears protrude. A large cross stood out against the white yoke of her dress beneath a dried-apple face. They said that during Sherman's invasion she had thrown a churn of buttermilk on the Yankee soldiers. Looking at her, Eliza was amazed the South had lost.

Pentecost Pitts, farmer, sometime-preacher, and little-known poet, had brought his bride, Lucy, back to Bellawood from South Carolina soon after the War Between the States. Here the couple raised corn, cotton and sorghum cane, plus three sons and five daughters whose dark portraits lined the walls of the drafty old house. And after he served his term as Georgia's governor in the latter part of the nineteenth century, it was at Bellawood that the industrious Captain Pitts wrote the dreadful verses that future school children of the community would be forced to memorize and quote with a straight face.

Eliza remembered trying not to look at Sydney as she stood before Miss Edna Blackstock's sixth grade to recite in a sing-song voice his tribute to Echota County.

> Deep brown rivers of my heart,
> Sweet green valleys of my soul,
> Quiet woodlands where I walk,
> Greater is thy worth than gold.
> (Greater is thy worth than gold.)

> And when angels call me home
> To that everlasting rest,
> May I know repose at last,
> Dear Echota, at thy breast.
> (Dear Echota at thy breast.)

Eliza's mother said that poem always made her cry, but to Eliza and her friends it had exactly the opposite effect. When you're eleven years old the word *breast* means one thing and one thing only. Twenty-seven children tried not to giggle. Two succeeded. Eliza never got over the agony of that experience, and she never forgave Pentecost Pitts for being responsible for it. And contrary to the poet's lofty ideals, his descendants must have found gold to be worthy enough as they eventually sold off more than six hundred acres of the old boy's land—valleys and woodlands included.

Now Eliza moved through the house as if it were her own, adjusting a dried arrangement in the dining room, filling a crockery bowl with rosy apples in the kitchen. Far removed from the sound of traffic, it was like living in another time, playing house in the pages of history. People had lived here, worked here, coped from day to day.
Bellawood was wired for electricity, but Eliza's small

office was the only room warmed by a wall unit. The rest of the house was heated by fireplaces. Today she wore a bulky sweater as she moved from room to room making sure Bellawood presented a respectable face to the public. With a feather duster, Eliza brushed a marble-topped table, the handsome hand-carved mantel. The old house made her feel curiously domestic. Her friends at the university wouldn't recognize her here.

Although she would never admit it aloud, Eliza loved Bellawood and sometimes pretended it was hers. The Pitts home was never a mansion, but a sturdy clapboard farmhouse that grew. At one time gingerbread trim was added to the wide front porch; a turret room, like a fancy wooden silo, tacked onto one corner. Eliza's office was in the round room upstairs where she could see who was coming and going.

Growing up in Minerva, Eliza and her friends had a long-standing joke about the name of the plantation:

"Bellawood."

"Bellawood what?"

"Bellawood . . . well . . . you know!"

Looking at the woman's stern features, it was hard for Eliza to believe that Bella would actually . . . *you know,* but she had produced four offspring to prove it.

A truck rumbled down the gravel road beside the house. From a back window Eliza was relieved to see Baxter Phillips in his familiar blue work clothes climb out, and with Abbott Yates, his wiry, close-mouthed assistant, remove a box of tools from the back.

Bellawood sat concealed among wooded acreage yards from the public road and more than five miles from town. And as much as Eliza felt at home there, the quiet sometimes bothered her. It bothered her today.

It had happened again last night. Eliza was shocked awake by Melody's terrified crying, and found her crouched in bed fighting with the covers, her eyes glassy with fear. "Go away! Leave me alone!" Melody's feet kicked the blue-flowered spread aside. A pillow hit the floor.

Eliza was afraid to touch her. "It's okay, Melody. It's just me—Eliza. Nobody's going to hurt you. Come on, now. Try to go back to sleep."

Finally she had crawled in beside her until Melody's long, shuddering sobbing subsided. Neither of them got much sleep.

Had Melody been abused as a child? Eliza couldn't remember her having such horrible nightmares when she stayed with the Figgs. And the Sutherlands didn't seem the type, but of course that didn't mean a thing. If it was true, Eliza was glad her mother would never know.

Even though the cold January sun was bright, Eliza found it hard to throw off the dregs of last night's frightening experience until the sound of hammering reminded her she had work to do too.

Still, Eliza wished she could see the workmen from her office window. It would make her feel less alone.

Phillips Construction, which Baxter and his father owned, was renovating the small stone chapel that sat in a grove of hardwoods at the back of the property. A devout Methodist, Pentecost Pitts didn't allow his family any excuses for not attending services. Even if it snowed, (which it rarely did) or if the creek rose, they walked in a body to sit in the solid, straight-backed pews and listen to the circuit-riding preacher hold forth every other Sunday.

Baxter had finished shoring up the building's foundations, and now he and Abbott Yates were reinforcing the roof before retiling. In an hour or so the two of them would bring Thermoses of coffee and join Eliza for a mid-morning break.

The phone rang in her office, and Eliza hurried upstairs to answer it. She hoped it wouldn't be her neighbor calling to announce that Melody was going to give birth to quadruplets or had some sort of serious complication with her pregnancy like Eliza's cousin Janice Jean. Janice Jean had had to go to bed and be waited on hand and foot, and currently was undergoing great suffering with number three.

Dorcas Youngblood had taken Melody to her doctor's appointment that morning, and Eliza was eager to hear what Dr. Epstein had to say.

"We're in luck!" Syd shouted in her usual earsplitting volume.

Eliza held the receiver at a distance. "Good, I could use some."

"Pamela Harrison says one of those units behind the A&P is empty," Sydney said.

Eliza frowned. "The A&P?"

"Apartments!" Syd screamed at her. "You know that block of rental property behind the A&P on Orchard Road? Well, one's vacant—furnished, too, I think."

"Oh," Eliza said. "Well . . ." From what she remembered about those apartments she wouldn't want to put anyone there, especially a sensitive young widow due to deliver her first child. "Aren't they kind of grim?"

"Well, they've fixed them up some, I think. Besides, she won't be there long. Anyway, Pamela says give her a call if you're interested."

Maybe she and Melody could look at the place after work, Eliza thought. Before it got too dark. But she knew she could never move Melody into one of the dismal units behind the A&P. Or anywhere else—not now.

Eliza sighed. Last January she had gone skiing with friends in Colorado. The year before, she and Spencer G. Fillmore had met in New York City for a dash-about winter holiday before he'd left to photograph village life in the Amazon River Basin. Since then she'd gotten two postcards and a collect phone call.

Eliza had scarcely hung up the phone before it rang again. This time she made a face as she recognized her neighbor's voice.

"Did that man ever get in touch with you?" Jessie Gilreath bellowed.

"What man?" Eliza absently scratched her arm, then

her neck. What was it about this woman that made her itch?

"Some man called out at Bellawood yesterday—it was my morning to greet, you know." Eliza could imagine Jessie patting her bright wad of hair. "Wanted to know if you worked out there. I think it had something to do with that woman staying over at your house. Said he was a relative of hers."

"Did he give you a name?" Eliza asked. "Does he want me to call him back?"

"Wouldn't say. Didn't leave a number. Kind of rude, I thought, after I ran up all them steps just to answer the phone." Jessie sighed long and hard, which was the only way she knew how to sigh. "Didn't know you were having company. Anybody I know?"

Eliza remembered the time Melody had picked Jessie's daffodils and sold them to the neighbors for a nickel apiece. She thought they would never hear the end of that. "I'll tell you about it later," she said, trying to sound like the no-nonsense businesswoman she wasn't. "Right now I'm just about covered up with work . . . thanks for calling, Mrs. Gilreath."

Eliza spent the next hour compiling material for a new brochure on Bellawood, which was a working farm supported by private funds and an enthusiastic group of volunteers. This afternoon docents would demonstrate fireplace cookery to a troop of Girl Scouts and the old house would smell of gingerbread and spiced cider. Tonight the Board of Directors would meet in the little back parlor where a fire was laid.

She was surprised when Baxter and his sidekick came clomping in for their break.

"Man, it's cold out there!" Baxter said, rubbing his hands together. "And not a hell of a lot warmer in this house."

"One of the docents should be here soon to start the kitchen fire," Eliza told him. The original kitchen had been in a cabin separate from the house, but later owners had joined it to the main building, and reconstructed the old brick chimney.

Abbott Yates took a gulp of coffee and looked at Eliza's messy desk, combing it with his sharp gray eyes, looking for something to eat. Eliza usually brought sticky buns from home or picked up doughnuts to tide them over till lunch.

"Sorry, no goodies today," Eliza said, wishing she had some herself. "Didn't have time to stop."

Baxter grinned. "Heard about your boarder."

"I wish you'd use another term," Eliza said.

"Think she'll be here long?" Baxter poured coffee into her chipped enamel mug and slid it in front of her with clean square-tipped fingers. His eyes were blue and friendly. Back in high school when Baxter Phillips had played right guard on the football team, Eliza and her friends had called him a "mean, mean sex machine," although she doubted if any of them could vouch for it. She knew she couldn't.

"I don't know what to think," she told him. "I'm sort of feeling my way through this one day at a time. Any suggestions?"

Eliza felt comfortable talking to Baxter. He knew the dreadful secrets of her past: That she had spit on Moose O'Donoghue in kindergarten, started a fight in the second grade, worn braces until she was thirteen. And on the afternoon of her fifteenth birthday, Baxter Phillips had witnessed the separation of Eliza from her bikini top when she did a back flip out at Indian Meadow Lake.

"You'll work it out," he said.

Baxter waited until Abbott had gone out for a cigarette before he continued. "Any chance of our going out Friday? 'Locomotive's' coming to Atlanta, and I thought we could get something to eat and take in the concert."

'Locomotive' was a country rock group, and although Eliza enjoyed some of their songs, she didn't want to sit through two hours of music that sounded like a train whistle.

Still, she did like Baxter. Their times together since she'd been home offered a welcome break from her mother's sickbed and the dreary weeks after her death.

In high school Eliza had sat behind him in algebra and memorized the line of his jaw and the way his hair grew around that little pink area just above his ears. She wondered what it would be like to nibble there.

Eliza glanced at Baxter's ears. Still tempting, but there was no way she could make plans for Friday. Melody was due any day. Oh, well! She shook her head. "Wish I could. If you change your mind about going, come by and I'll make lasagna—unless I'm holding Melody's hand in the hospital."

Baxter grinned, zipping his jacket on the way out. He paused at the door, searching his pockets for gloves. "What do you hear from your dad?"

Eliza came close to sneering. "A postcard from Miami, that's all."

"You're lucky to get that. Most people don't go in for letter writing on their honeymoon. And I've seen his new wife. What a knockout!"

Eliza's face burned. The words *honeymoon* and *new wife* didn't go with the word *dad.* She remembered her parents dancing to the radio in the kitchen, how her mother had sat on her dad's lap while watching a scary movie on television. And once when she was in high school she had come home early from a date and interrupted their lovemaking upstairs. At seventeen Eliza had been shocked and embarrassed that these two middle-aged people who had done their duty by having her should even think of such a thing. And in broad open daylight yet!

And what was she going to do about Melody? She couldn't handle this thing alone. Damn it! Why couldn't Benjamin Figg act his age and come back home where he belonged?

Baxter stood in the doorway with a remnant of a smile on his face. He looked as though he had forgotten something. "By the way, did that man ever find you?" he asked.

Eliza frowned. She was still furious with him for reminding her of her sexy stepmother. "What man? Jessie said somebody called yesterday—somebody looking for Melody, I guess. Did you talk with him too?"

"Drove up just after noon yesterday," Baxter said. "Abbott had gone to get hamburgers, and I was waiting here for the guy to deliver those shingles. Wanted to know where you were. Said he was trying to locate his Cousin Melody."

"What did you tell him?"

"Hell, I didn't know who he was. Figured if he really wanted to find you, he'd call you later at home. I didn't tell him a damn thing!"

"Funny. Melody didn't mention anybody calling, but she probably wasn't at home either. She and Dorcas went to the mall to pick up some last minute baby things and stopped somewhere for lunch." Eliza set her empty mug aside. She was almost sure Melody had told her she didn't have any relatives.

"What did this man look like?" she asked.

"Fairly young, I think. Didn't get a good look at him; I was on the other side of that turnaround out there, and he had on some kind of cap."

Eliza ripped yesterday's page from her calendar and crushed it into a ball. She didn't like where this was going. "His car? Did you get a look at his car?"

Baxter shrugged. "Couldn't miss it. One of those big black Chryslers—been around awhile. Looked like a damned hearse!"

When the phone rang. Eliza jumped as if the big bad man in the black car were huffing and puffing at her door.

"You'd better get over here," Dorcas Youngblood said. "I think it's time."

"Time for what?" Eliza remembered Melody's appointment with Dr. Epstein and looked at her watch. Melody should have been there over an hour ago! "My gosh, was I supposed to take her? I thought you were—"

"Eliza, calm down and listen." Her neighbor's voice was steady, reminding Eliza of the time she was eight and cut her foot on a piece of broken glass while her mother was visiting next door, and Eliza had run crying in the house, trailing blood across her neighbor's living room rug.

"I'm calling from the *clinic*," Dorcas emphasized the last word. "Melody's water broke and they're rushing her to the hospital in an ambulance. Dr. Epstein is with her— don't worry."

"Her water broke? "Does that mean . . . ?"

"It means the baby is on the way," Dorcas said, laughing. "It means you'd better high-tail it over to the hospital right now, Eliza Figg!"

All the way to Echota General Hospital Eliza thought about bottles. Weren't you supposed to have bottles? She hadn't seen a one. Melody planned to breast feed, she knew, but babies had to have water too, didn't they? And juice. She wasn't sure about that other stuff—slimy bananas and gloppy green peas that came in jars.

The bassinet, along with the necessary linens, waited beside Melody's bed. They had planned to give it a fresh coat of paint and weave a ribbon through its wicker sides; no time for that now.

Dorcas waited in the lobby, with its sagging green furniture and the same five seascape prints that had been on the wall forever. Together they went upstairs to that little room where expectant fathers were supposed to pace. Melody was in the delivery room, Dorcas told her, and probably would be for a good long time—this being the first one.

Sometime in the middle of the afternoon Eliza's stomach rumbled. She glanced at her watch and tossed aside the dog-eared copy of *Reader's Digest* she was scanning for the second time. "No wonder I'm hungry! It's almost four and I haven't had lunch."

"Come to think of it, neither have I." Dorcas crammed quilting scraps into her bulging carpetbag and got to her feet. "Let's see if the cafeteria's open."

It wasn't. But the snack shop was. Eliza had just taken her first bite of what she thought was a pimento cheese sandwich when a young Candy Striper poked her shaggy dandelion head in the door and grinned. "Thought I'd find you here," she said.

Eliza almost choked on a swallow of water. "What is it? What's wrong? Has the baby come?"

"Seven pounds, four ounces!" The girl beamed as if she had delivered the baby herself. "Mother's doing fine . . . oh, and Dr. Epstein will meet you in the waiting room." She turned and flounced away.

Eliza looked at her neighbor as they gathered their things together. "Did I miss something, or did she forget to tell us if it's a boy or a girl?"

Chapter Six

"Misty Dawn," Melody said, sipping Coca-Cola over chipped ice. She shifted the straw to get the last swallow.

"Misty dawn what?" Eliza glanced out at a wet January night.

"For her name, the baby's name. What do you think?"

"Sounds like a cheap perfume," Eliza said. "You asked."

Dorcas made a face. "Or a feminine hygiene product: *For that refreshing, confident feeling, try Misty Dawn, available in pine, mint, and apple blossom at drugstores everywhere . . .*" Dorcas looked down at the tiny white-wrapped bundle in her arms and kissed the top of the baby's head. "We won't let her do that to you, honey."

Melody shifted against her pillows and retied the pink ribbon in her hair. She wore the lilac quilted bed jacket Martha Figg had worn after Eliza's birth in that same hospital. It smelled of cedar and lavender sachet.

"Well, I'd thought of Brandi Nicole, but I don't

51

know . . ." Melody looked from one to the other. "Frankly, Sonny and I were sort of counting on a boy."

Eliza caught her neighbor's eye and looked away. Bite your tongue, she told herself. It's not your baby.

But Dorcas had no such qualms. "Well, she'll have a lot of company," she said, covering the baby's tiny wrinkled foot. "At least every other young'un born in Echota County in the last five years is named either Brandi or Nicole—sometimes both. For the life of me I can't figure out this fascination with alcoholic beverages and soap opera stars!" Gently she rocked the nameless infant. "Why don't you give the child a good, solid family name? Give her some roots to hang onto."

Did Melody's lip quiver? Eliza moved to the bedside and smoothed the mirror-starched sheet. "That jacket looks good on you, Melody. My gosh, you look even younger than you did before. If this keeps up, you and the baby can start nursery school together."

Good, the beginning of a smile! "You said you were counting on a boy. Were you going to name the baby for Sonny?"

Melody nodded, teary-eyed again. "So the name wouldn't die." She stretched out her arms for the baby and stroked her downy cheek with one finger.

"A lot of women I know are named for their fathers," Eliza reminded her. "My friend Sydney, for example. And just think of all the Tommies and Billies and Gerries."

"I had a college roommate named Clyde." Dorcas grinned. "Now that was way *before* they had coed dorms."

"You see—you could still name the baby for her daddy." Eliza stepped back and waited. "What was Sonny's name?"

"Horace." Melody's smile turned into a giggle. "Horace Witherspoon Lamb III. Now you know why I called him Sonny."

Melody's cheeks seemed pinker, fuller, and her eyes were less haggard. This is what her mother meant, Eliza thought, remembering how Martha Figg had used the term when speaking of a bride or an expectant mother. *She glows.* The Melody Lamb sitting there in bed with her day-old baby girl barely resembled the wet, frightened refugee of a few days ago. Maybe she was going to act like a normal person, after all.

"Would you like to hold her?" Melody said. "It's kind of nice—really. Come on."

Eliza blinked. Was she talking to *her?* She moved as close to the bed as she could and let Melody shift the limp cocoon into her arms. She had held babies before— of course she had. But none this small, this boneless.

The baby made sort of a soft grunting sound like a little piglet and kicked her bare feet. She had funny looking feet: little comma-shaped feet that looked as if they'd been soaking in water too long.

Melody sat up straighter. "Oh, I wish Sonny could've seen her. She's perfect, just perfect! And so pretty too."

What could she say? Eliza glanced at Dorcas, but Dorcas was looking at the child through an adoring misty-eyed glaze. "Beautiful," Dorcas said.

Eliza looked down at the pink splotched face and puffy eyes. A reddish-brown tuft of hair sprouted on an otherwise bald head. The baby looked like a little old man with a bad hangover.

"She sure does smell good," Eliza said, avoiding the mother's eyes. She wondered if it would be all right to shift positions some. Her arm was getting numb.

"Here, let me hold her." Dorcas scooped the infant onto her shoulder. "I just can't get enough of her. Pity you didn't have twins, Melody, so Eliza and I wouldn't have to share."

"Twins! Oh God, no!" Melody looked as if she thought a great stork might swoop into the room and dump another little old gnome into her lap. "What an awful thought! I don't need another one to fight with her and make her cry and take away her toys. One is enough!"

"I used to think it would be kind of fun to be a twin,"

Eliza said. "You'd always have somebody to play with, and you could wear each other's clothes—and play tricks on people."

"Ugh! No thanks." Melody pressed a button, lowering the top of her bed. Suddenly she seemed tired. "I've been thinking, Eliza. If you don't care . . . well, I'd kind of like to name the baby for your mother—and for mine."

"Care?" Eliza smiled. "Why should I care? I think It's a great idea, and I know Mama would love it."

"What was your mother's name?" Dorcas asked Melody.

"I don't know my natural mother's name, but I sort of remember her face. She was blond, I think. And pretty." Melody yawned. "But my other mother's name is Susan. She and your mom were the only mothers I knew. What do you think of Martha Susan?"

"Martha Susan Lamb. A fine substantial name. I like it. It's feminine, yet it has dignity. Backbone." Dorcas smiled as she tucked the baby beside her mother. Soon the nurse would come and whisk her back to the nursery.

"Martha Susan. That's quite a handle for somebody who's not much bigger than my Granddaddy Winston's nose," Eliza said.

Melody snuggled her daughter closer. "That's okay. We'll call her Mattie." She lay back with the infant against her face and closed her eyes. It made her look childlike and vulnerable. And for a minute Eliza thought Melody had drifted off to sleep until she stirred slightly and turned toward the window. Melody's large greenish eyes had a defeated look, as if she were frightened of something, yet resigned to it.

"Promise me something, Eliza . . ." Melody stared at the black square of night where a plane's lights winked red and green in the distance. "If anything should happen to me, promise you'll take care of Mattie."

"Oh, come on! What've they been giving you in here, morbid pills? Don't be silly!"

Eliza glanced in desperation at Dorcas who shook her head. "Postnatal blues," Dorcas said. "It'll pass."

"No! No, I mean it! Promise me—*please!*" Melody spoke in such shrieking tones Eliza was afraid she would alarm the other patients.

She hurried to take her hand, to calm her. "Of course I will, Melody, but you'll never have to worry about that. Now, try to get some rest."

Melody fixed her with her dug-in, bullheaded look and squeezed her hand. Hard. "You promise?"

"I promise," Eliza said. The baby made a face in her sleep.

The next morning when Eliza went out to get the paper, she saw Jessie Gilreath coming up the walk with one of her lemonade pies. Eliza knew it was a lemonade pie. That was the only kind Jessie ever made: frozen lemonade, condensed milk, and whipped topping in a graham cracker crust was her neighbor's passport to snoop.

Ben Figg once reckoned that if the stores were to run out of those ingredients it would put an end to Jessie's solicitous visits because she didn't have enough imagination to gather her information any other way.

But Eliza knew that Jessie spied. Whenever anyone in the neighborhood entertained, Jessie would make it a point to water her flowers or prune the four round box-woods like huge green bowling balls that bordered her front walk. And in high school, Eliza and her dates had delighted in frustrating her neighbor by necking on the porch behind the dark oak foliage.

"Thought you might be able to use this since you've got another mouth to feed," Jessie said. She thrust the plastic-wrapped plate at Eliza, and stood there waiting to be invited in; stood there looking at Eliza with her little glinty brown eyes. Mean eyes. "Any news yet?" Jessie tried to peer past Eliza into the hall. "Saw that woman drive off with Dorcas Youngblood the other day. Looked like she was fixing to deliver any minute."

Might as well tell her now, Eliza thought, stepping back to let her neighbor inside. She'll find out anyway.

It took almost half an hour, a couple of applesauce muffins, and two cups of spiced tea to explain Melody's predicament to her neighbor's satisfaction, and another five minutes to get her to the door.

Jessie hesitated on the threshold. "By the way, what do you hear from your daddy?"

"I expect them back any day now." The *them* stuck in her throat.

"Been too busy to write, I reckon." Jessie attempted a smile. It made her look as if she'd been surprised by a gas pain.

Jessie Gilreath wasn't the only one who made jokes about Ben Figg's quick marriage to the widow from Atlanta. Eliza sensed when people grew suddenly quiet as she entered a room, or changed the topic of conversation in a much-too-hearty manner, that they had been talking about her father. She really didn't blame them. If it had been somebody else's father, she would have reacted the same way. Her daddy must have been unbearably lonely to have done what he did.

Eliza watched brown leaves chase one another across the front walk after Jessie Gilreath left. The two big ferns on either side of the front door were dead because she had forgotten to bring them inside last fall, and the porch chairs leaned, rockers up, against the wall for the season. The house was filled with a bleak winter silence.

But not for long. Tomorrow Melody would arrive with the new baby, and Eliza had a long list of things to do. Today she had to hurry if she meant to get to work on time. Surely the excitement of coming home with a new baby would sweep away Melody's gloomy mood. A lot of new mothers get depressed, Dorcas had assured her. Nothing to worry about. Still, Eliza wished she could shove Melody's melodramatic request from her mind.

* * *

It was dark as Eliza drove back from the hospital that night. Earlier, she and Sydney, with Syd's husband Eddie, had wrestled the baby crib from the attic and set it up in Melody's room. Funny how she already thought of it as Melody's room.

The baby bed that had been Katherine's, then hers, and later held her sister's two children, was scrubbed antiseptic clean and spread with Mother Goose linens. A colorful mobile, a present from Syd, dangled above it.

Since her mother's death, Eliza dreaded returning at night to the empty house. Her parents had liked to entertain, and had often invited friends to share whatever good things baked or simmered in the big kitchen.

Eliza missed the music and the laughter. Martha Figg had studied voice in college and was frequently asked to sing at weddings. For thirty years she sat in the third chair on the left in the soprano section of Sequoyah Street Presbyterian Church. She sang when she washed dishes, or swept the porch, or shelled peas. And she laughed her delicate soap bubble laugh. Martha Figg could never tell a joke without breaking up before the punch line.

Often during those late summer evenings when her father retired to his room to brood in silence, Eliza would sit and remember the laughter, the singing, the good smells coming from the kitchen. She wondered sometimes if laughter lives on after a person dies, because once in a while she thought she heard the echo of her mother's chiming voice, and for a while was reassured.

Tonight as Eliza turned onto Habersham Street, she wished she had remembered to leave a light on in the hall so she wouldn't have to come home to a dark house. But as she got closer she was surprised to see not only the hall light burning, but the whole downstairs yellow-lit. Her father's dark blue Chevrolet stood in the driveway.

CHAPTER SEVEN

liza could see their silhouettes in the living room: her father, tall and straight backed, walked restlessly about, while the woman—that woman who was not her mother—stood with her back to the window. Talking, probably. She was good at that. She had talked Benjamin Figg all the way to the altar, hadn't she?

Her father had met Olivia O'Shea in September, when at his family's urging, he finally agreed to spend a few days in Atlanta with an old college friend. The friend, whom Eliza had always trusted, and even called "Uncle Willie," had invited a few neighbors over for dinner and bridge. Olivia was among them. This was the same "Uncle Willie" who had called her mother "Princess Tea Cake" for some silly reason, and had showered her with candy, flowers, and flattery for as long as Eliza could remember.

Eliza knew Uncle Willie's intentions were good, but what was meant to be an evening of pleasant diversion, turned into something a lot more serious, and a few days turned into a week.

Before long, her father began to neglect the hardware and garden supply business he had worked so hard to develop over the years, until his partner, C. C. Reece, was doing most of the work.

Meanwhile, Ben Figg almost wore out a new set of tires going back and forth to court the widow O'Shea. At first Eliza teased him about her. "You must have finally found somebody who will let you beat them at Scrabble . . . or else she makes one hell of a pecan pie!" Pecan pie was Ben Figg's favorite dessert, and Eliza pictured a chubby, rosy-cheeked matron who spent hours in the kitchen with flour smudges on her face.

Not so. Not only was his new "friend" beautiful, but she had the daintiest feet and the smallest waist of any woman he knew, Benjamin Figg claimed.

And that was what shoved Eliza over the edge. It was bad enough that a man her father's age was making a complete ass of himself, but for the object of his affections to be in better shape than she was, was more than Eliza could stand.

On Thanksgiving Day Ben Figg announced to his family that he and the diminutive Olivia would marry at Christmastime. Eliza's sister Katherine had driven all the way from Virginia with her family to help make the holiday as normal as possible for their recently widowed father. The family sat at Martha Figg's table and ate from her violet patterned china a traditional Thanksgiving dinner made from her familiar recipes.

Eliza had just served the ambrosia and Japanese fruit cake when her father divulged his bit of news, and her sister left the table without saying a word and wouldn't come out of her room for three hours. Eliza, who had never known Katherine to leave even a spoonful of ambrosia uneaten, was almost as stunned over her sister's reaction as she was at her father's announcement. Since that time the little town of Minerva, Georgia, had followed the proceedings open-mouthed.

Eliza parked behind her father's car, turned off the engine and sat in the dark. She wasn't ready for this. What would she say? Was she expected to embrace the new Mrs. Figg? She wondered if they had seen the crib upstairs, the bassinet in the living room, the bottles and plastic baby tub (borrowed from Syd) on the kitchen counter. Maybe they would think they were hers. Eliza smiled. Good! Let them.

Ben Figg threw open the door and grabbed her before she could cross the porch, wrapping his long arms around her as he always did, and smelling as he always did of that wonderful woodsy aftershave.

"What's all this baby paraphernalia lying about?" Her father chuckled. "Olivia was scared to death. Thought you expected us to produce an offspring or something." He reached for his bride's hand and pulled her to him, kissing the perfect silky curl over her forehead. "You know you did, admit it, Livvy!"

Ben Figg's jovial face became serious when Eliza told him about Melody. "You mean *little* Melody? *Our* Melody? Sure sounds like she's had a tough time of it. Awful thing to happen!" He squeezed his daughter's hand. "I'm glad you were here for her, honey."

Eliza nodded, afraid to speak. The tears were in her throat, working their way up and out. That's right, she wanted to say. Lean on me, everybody. Get in line. I'm here to serve. Maybe she could have cards printed.

They filed into the sitting room, dusty and cluttered. A poinsettia from Christmas sat on a table by the window amid a scattering of dead leaves. Three or four tenacious petals clung to the stem. Melody's fuzzy pink slippers lay on the rug where she'd kicked them three days before.

Olivia perched lightly in the armchair by the fireplace where cold black ashes stirred in a draft from the chimney. She sat like an excited little girl waiting her turn at a piano recital. "Will she stay long, do you think?" Olivia asked.

"Probably for a couple of months until she can find a place of her own," Eliza said.

Ben Figg slapped his bony knees. "Well, she can stay as long as she likes as far as I'm concerned. This house is yours, honey, as long as you want to live here. You know that, don't you? Frankly, I'm glad you're here. Much rather it be you than some tenant who wouldn't take care of the place."

"Remember when I had a life of my own? Whatever happened to that, I wonder?" Eliza would discuss *taking care of the place later.* Did he not even notice the splotched wallpaper in the hall?

"Eliza, honey, I know you're unhappy right now, but things will work out. You don't have to stay in Minerva, you know—not if you don't want to. But since you're here, I'm glad you could help Melody. Sounds like she needs it."

"Where was Melody living before she came here as a child?" Eliza asked.

"I think she stayed in a series of foster homes after her mother gave her up." Her father frowned. "Until the last couple—the one she was with the longest—well, seems the family broke up, started divorce proceedings. Then for a while it looked like she might be adopted, but the people changed their minds at the last minute . . . and there she was, practically a baby: five or six at the most, and nowhere to go. It was just before Christmas, remember?"

Eliza nodded. "She seems different now. Moody—almost neurotic. I don't remember her being this way."

"Are you sure it's the same person?" Olivia asked. "How long has it been since you've seen her? It *is* Melody, isn't it?"

"Of course it is, Livvy," her husband said. "My God, think what she's been through!"

"And the baby . . ." Olivia swung a tiny suede-clad foot and paused to dig inside her elegant tapestry handbag before snapping it shut again. Apparently she didn't find what she wanted. "You're going to get attached to this baby, Eliza," Olivia said. "When the time comes, it might be difficult to see them go."

I'll try to manage. Eliza made herself smile. Her face felt as if it were cast in plaster. "Oh, I imagine they'll keep in touch. I don't expect they'll be going very far." Sydney had warned her about that same thing earlier. But she would be at Bellawood all day, Eliza told her, and babies slept at night, didn't they? Besides, Melody and little Mattie wouldn't be here long enough for Eliza to become accustomed to them.

"I remember how hard it was for us when Melody left," Ben said. "Why, it was like giving up part of the family. Took your mother the longest time to get over that."

"The baby's named for Mama," Eliza told him. "Martha Susan. She's calling her Mattie." She looked at Olivia who smiled while fingering the catch on her purse, and at her father who seemed to be examining the hooked rug at his feet. "Your mama would like that," he said finally.

Eliza excused herself and almost ran to the kitchen where she turned on the faucet full force, hoping the drumming of the water would cover the sound of her crying.

Ben Figg allowed her a few minutes before he followed. She felt his hand on her arm.

"Honey, this is hard on you, I know. I hate to leave you like this." He backed away, looking oddly out of place in his own house.

"Leave? Where are you going? I've made up the bed." *Mama's bed.*

"We have to get on back to Atlanta, Baby. Livvy's got me taking tennis lessons—believe it or not. First class starts in the morning."

Tennis! The last time her father played tennis was when Eliza was in junior high and needed someone to hit balls with so she could improve her chances for the tennis team. As it turned out, she was better at it than he was, and she still didn't make the team.

"But what about the store?" Had he forgotten he had a business to run?

"Well, that's one thing we came to tell you. C. C. and I have talked about it, and 'Liza, I'm going to sell him my share of the business."

"What?" Eliza gripped the back of a chair—one of the old-fashioned drugstore chairs. She had helped her mother paint them white only a couple of years ago.

"You know Olivia has a decorating business down in the Virginia Highlands area . . . a lot of new people moving into that part of Atlanta, and now we've had a chance to buy the little frame shop next door."

"Frame shop?" What did her father know about a frame shop?

"The fellow who's selling the place has agreed to stay for a while at least—just until I become familiar with it." Ben Figg beamed as if he had discovered the reason for being.

"How nice," Eliza said.

"You wouldn't?" Dorcas said the next day. "You really wouldn't have all that work done on the house without checking first with your father! I know you're upset with your daddy, Eliza, but you don't want to see him in debt. . . .

". . . do you?" Dorcas shook her head. "Oh, Eliza, how sharper than a snake's tongue to have a thankless child!"

"That's serpent's tooth, Dorcas. You must have been thinking about Jessie Gilreath. Now *she* has a sharp tongue. And I did say something to him, caught him right between tennis and golf this morning. Seems Olivia can get us a deal on some of those things—like wallpaper and paint. She's in the decorating business, you know." Eliza shrugged. "At least she's good for something."

Eliza had taken a long lunch hour to bring Melody and

the baby home from the hospital. Both had been fed and snugly tucked in for a nap, and Dorcas would be staying with them until Eliza got home from work.

Since the next day was Saturday, Eliza was expected to stay at home with them all day and the thought terrified her. She would have to bathe that limp, slippery little red thing. What if she dropped her? Stuck her with a pin? Oh, God! What had she gotten herself into?

And what if Olivia's suggestion turned out to be true, and Melody Lamb was really somebody else? But why would anyone pretend to be Melody? The Sutherlands didn't have any money. As far as Eliza knew, their daughter wouldn't come into any great inheritance.

Besides, this fragile young waif/mother looked like Melody. After Olivia and Ben left the night before, Eliza had searched through old photograph albums until she found several pictures made during the time Melody stayed with the Figgs. The delicate child's face had grown to adult proportions, and she wore her straight brown hair a different way, but she looked like Melody. She *was* Melody! Wasn't she?

Later, as Eliza returned to Bellawood, she was tempted to just keep on driving—past the hedge of crape myrtle that bordered the farm, past the golf course at the end of town, the abandoned school with broken windows. She would take a room under an assumed name in some fun place—like Savannah or Daytona Beach. No one would find her there.

Earlier that morning Baxter Phillips had invited Eliza to a party at his parents' mountain cabin. If they were lucky, he said, they might get snow. He had seemed disappointed when she had to turn him down, even pouted a little.

Eliza wondered who Baxter would ask in her place. She wondered if it would snow and hoped it wouldn't. She wondered if he would understand and ask her out again.

How could such a tiny baby—somebody else's baby—

be like an anchor dragging behind her, holding her down?

But it wouldn't be for long. She had talked with Melody the day before. She wanted to be independent, Melody said, to have a place of her own, and eventually go back to work. It would only be for a little while: a couple of months at the most. Tonight Eliza would write her professor in California and tell him to look for her next quarter. With luck she would soon take up where she had left off with her life. Maybe she would even look up Spencer G. Fillmore.

California, here I come! Eliza smiled as she turned into the gates at Bellawood. By the middle of March she would be free. The Ides of March. For Caesar it was a date to beware, but not for Eliza Figg.

CHAPTER EIGHT

"Good Lord, it's hot for June." Syd let the screen door bounce shut behind her. "Aren't you about to melt in here? Something wrong with your air conditioner?"

"Melody says it makes her cold. Here, sit down." Eliza gathered an armload of freshly dried baby clothes from the end of the sofa and dumped them onto a chair. They smelled warm and sunny and still bore the imprint of the wooden clothespins where Melody had clamped them on the line.

"How is Melody?" Sydney sat down with a groan and fanned herself with yesterday's newspaper. "Still acting weird?"

"Better . . . I think, at least on the days she works at Bellawood. Came in one day last week, though, looking like the devil himself was right on her tail. Had that scary expression: you know, where her face gets all tight and funny."

"Did she tell you why?"

"Didn't want to talk about it." Eliza folded a dainty

batiste smock and added it to a stack of embroidered diaper shirts. "Something has her hackles up, though. Know what she said?

"Wanted to know if a person is aware when they're losing their mind."

"Ask any mother of twins!" Sydney sat up straighter, laying the newspaper aside with a final plop. "Why? Does Melody think she's going nuts?"

"Asked me if mental illness was inherited, if I knew anything about her parents—her natural parents: the ones who put her up for adoption." Eliza shrugged. "I don't, of course. We never saw them. I don't even know who they were."

"It isn't the man in the black car, is it?" Syd asked. "Has he been calling again?"

"Not that I know of. She didn't mention it. But she's started having those awful nightmares, cries like a scared little girl. Says somebody's trying to hurt her. Wish I could get her to a doctor, but she won't go."

"Do you think something happened when she was little? Something she's suppressed?"

"I don't know. I thought of that, but she says not," Eliza said. "Melody will be okay for a while, and then— *bam!* She's off on one of her tangents. If I didn't know better, I'd think she was on something."

"On something? You mean like drugs? How do you know she isn't?"

Eliza smoothed the little pile of clothing and set it aside. "Melody's too good a mother to risk harming Mattie. Still nursing, you know. Besides, she doesn't have the money. It's just that—well, sometimes I think she's hallucinating, seeing things."

Sydney frowned. "What do you mean? What kind of things?"

"Well, not things, really. People. People who aren't there."

"You're giving me the creeps, Eliza. Sounds like Melody needs to see a shrink. Who is she supposed to have seen? Does she say?"

"Not exactly, just that it was somebody who wasn't supposed to be there. It really shook her up."

"You mean like a person who died? Maybe she thinks she's seeing her husband . . . what's his name? Sonny. Sometimes when people are grieving, they'll swear they've seen or heard the person who died. Don't guess there's anything abnormal about that." Syd stood and started looking for her car keys, digging under the sofa cushions, shoving aside magazines on the coffee table.

"I know. I saw a woman who looked so much like Mama the other day it made my throat close up," Eliza said. "She was coming down the street with a little bag of groceries—even walked like Mama. I just about had a wreck."

"He *is* dead, isn't he? Sonny?" Syd finally found her keys at the bottom of her ancient leather handbag.

Eliza nodded. "Melody had to identify him. But that could be it, I guess. After all, he hasn't been dead a year, and grief has done stranger things than that. Not long ago she woke up crying—said she was afraid she was going to hurt herself. Worries me."

Syd looked at her watch and sat back down fingering the clump of keys. "Have you ever wondered if maybe there wasn't a Sonny?"

"What? Why would you say that?"

"Think about it," Syd said. "There was nothing in her apartment that belonged to him—nothing! And have you ever seen a photograph of Sonny Lamb?"

"But she gave his things away. They made her sad, she said. That's why she doesn't keep his picture on display . . ." Eliza felt a tickle of a shiver. "Oh Lord, Sydney! You don't suppose . . . No! Wait a minute—there's the insurance. Melody had Sonny's insurance policy. I saw it myself. There had to be a Sonny."

Syd shrugged. "I hope you're right. Where is Melody, by the way?"

"Out looking for a day care center. A good one. She can't keep dragging Mattie around with her, and we're running out of sitters."

"What about Penny Shillinglaw? I know she's saving for a car." Syd went over and looked at Mattie who rooted happily in the playpen; saliva dripped from her chin. "Teething," she said.

"And trying to crawl—see? She wants to so bad." Eliza knew she sounded just like those obnoxious young mothers she had always tried to avoid, but she couldn't help it. Mattie didn't even resemble that ugly little Martian they had brought home from the hospital, and she did seem advanced for her age. Eliza didn't remember her sister's children making such intelligent noises. "Penny's okay once in a while," she said. "Melody's used her some—when she couldn't get anybody else, but I wouldn't want to have to rely on her. Too boy crazy. Dorcas saw her flirting with the Phylers' house painter one day when she had Mattie out in the stroller. And she's always on the phone. Wouldn't surprise me if one grew to her ear."

"She is a silly little twit," Syd said. "You just have to lay down the rules: no telephone, no boyfriends, and no ordering pizza. She knows she has to stay in line at my house. My kids talk."

Eliza wiped the baby's chin and checked her diaper. "Penny must have a crush on one of those men remodeling the Phyler house. She jogs by here at least three times a day in shorts up to her 'possible' and one of those see-through nylon tank tops."

Sydney giggled at their old joke about the woman who took the "spit" bath. She washed down as far as possible, she said, and up as far as possible. Then she washed "possible."

"We only need somebody a few hours a day," Eliza went on. "Melody doesn't earn enough to pay much, but working has been good for her. She's happier when she's busy."

"They've been needing something like this out at Bellawood," Syd said. "The docents are excited about finally having a place to eat lunch, and even Jessie Gilreath admitted Melody made the best pound cake she had ever put in her mouth."

In the five months since her baby was born, Melody had looked at a couple of apartments, and had even answered one or two advertisements for jobs, but nothing seemed right. She appeared to be perfectly content to take care of Mattie and browse through the recipes in her tower of cookbooks. Melody seemed a fraction away from *happy* in the kitchen.

Eliza became accustomed to coming home from work to a deep dish chicken pie or beef burgundy with fluffy white rice. But Melody's specialty was desserts. Wonderful desserts, like English trifle with almonds and sherry, cherry cobbler with a hint of nutmeg, and gingerbread dripping in hot lemon sauce. According to her reflection in the mirror, Eliza's face seemed a little rounder than before, and she was aware that her waistbands were getting snugger. So far she hadn't even had the nerve to try on the shorts from the previous summer.

It had been Dorcas who suggested that Melody put her cooking ability to work at Bellawood. The farm needed a place for guests to get a light lunch or a snack, and a few coats of paint and some minor repairs had converted the small brick guest house on the property into Bella's Tea Room. For the last few weeks, Melody had been happily dispensing soup, sandwiches and pastries to the homestead's hungry sightseers.

Mattie began to fret, and Eliza picked her up and raised her to her shoulder. She smelled like apple juice and baby powder.

"Do you think Melody will stick it out?" Syd said.

"Why not? At least it gives her a little income and some time away from the baby—as much as she wants, anyway. Later, when Mattie's older, she'll probably want to move on to something more profitable. She's talked about starting a catering business."

"God knows, we need one." Syd looked at her watch. "Wish somebody'd cater my supper." She laughed as Mattie drooled on Eliza's beige linen sheath. "Look at you. I can't believe this. You realize, don't you, that dress will have to go to the cleaners?"

Eliza shrugged. "Haven't had time to change."

"No, and I don't suppose you've had time for anything else lately either—like a love life." Sydney frowned. "When was the last time you went out with Baxter?"

"Oh, I don't know . . . couple of weeks ago I guess."

"Couple of weeks, my foot. It was when you went to that play with Eddie and me. That was almost six weeks ago, Eliza. Hasn't he even called?"

"Hush, you'll scare the baby. Sure he's called. I was busy. Next time I'll tell him to go through my social secretary since you've obviously taken on the job."

"Suit yourself." Syd stood to go. "I just don't want to see you hurt. Melody isn't going to stay here forever, you know. As soon as she can afford it, she'll find her own place. And she should."

"So?" Eliza patted the baby's fat leg.

"I think you know what I mean," Syd said. The softness of her voice was startling.

Eliza wished Syd would get off the subject of Baxter Phillips. Syd would like nothing better than for Eliza to marry Baxter and settle down in Minerva. And sometimes Eliza was jealous of her friend's domestic harmony, her obvious contentment with her family and her big old rambling house. But Eliza wasn't ready yet—why, she wasn't even thirty. Sure, she might get married someday. But it wouldn't be to Baxter Phillips.

Eliza shifted the baby to one hip and followed Syd to the porch, glad for the deep shade of the big oak that at least gave the illusion of coolness. The red petunias by the front walk drooped in the sun, although it was nearly six o'clock.

Sydney frowned against the glare as Jessie Gilreath trundled her wheelbarrow around the yard a few houses down the street. "What's that woman doing now? Gonna have a heat stroke out there."

"Looks like she's putting in a new crop of impatiens," Eliza said, pausing on the steps. "The first planting died—too much sun, but Jessie won't listen. Knows everything."

"Her geraniums look pretty good," Syd said. "Maybe she'd better stick to those."

"What geraniums?"

"The red ones in that upstairs window box. Nice color. They look healthy enough."

Eliza laughed. "Ought to, they're plastic."

"You're kidding! How do you know?"

"Dorcas was the one who noticed it. They didn't change, she said. Just stayed in the same place, so we kept an eye on them for a couple of weeks: same as ever." Eliza sat on the step and balanced Mattie on one knee. "And then a couple of days later when Melody was out walking the baby, she saw her at the window up there moving them around. It was early in the morning before everybody leaves for work; guess Jessie didn't think anybody'd see her."

"Competing for 'Lawn of the Week,' no doubt. We'll see the old hag's picture in the *Minerva Mercury* grinning for all the world with that silly cow plop on her head!"

Syd stooped to take Mattie's hand. "You are adorable, 'Fat Stuff!' I can see how you've turned your Aunt Eliza into a marshmallow." She hoisted her large pocketbook to the other shoulder. "Gotta go! It's been a long day. Melody must have endless energy to get up and walk as early as that."

"Well, it's cooler then," Eliza said. "And I think it's become one of her little rituals. She takes Mattie out at the same time every morning, unless it's raining. Melody does things a certain way, you know—like the baby's laundry. Did you know she hand washes all of Mattie's things? Irons them too, except for diapers, of course."

Sydney smiled. "Like playing dolls. I did that with my

first one. Now I just toss the clean clothes into a basket and grab out whatever's handy."

Eliza sat in the porch swing with Mattie for a while after Sydney left. The motion seemed to lull the baby. Dorcas Youngblood called to them and waved as she watered her hanging baskets next door. And right on schedule, Penny Shillinglaw came trotting down the sidewalk, earphones clamped to her shaggy yellow head. A few minutes later, Eliza heard The Boss bark in excitement as Penny let herself in the gate to feed him as she usually did when the dog's owners were out of town. Except for the Thornbroughs, Penny Shillinglaw was about the only person who wasn't afraid of The Boss. Eliza didn't know why her neighbors got the dog in the first place. They never seemed to show him any attention and kept him confined in that small backyard with little opportunity to run. In a way, she couldn't blame him for having a nasty disposition. Still, Eliza was glad for the fence between them.

She was just going inside to mix the baby's cereal when Melody turned in the driveway. "Well, Miss Mattie, looks like you'll have your dinner on time after all," Eliza said. You could always count on Melody to be punctual.

Eliza had encouraged Melody to make friends her own age, and tried to introduce her to the few that she knew. "You must get tired of seeing nobody but me," Eliza suggested. "Syd has a neighbor with a little boy just about Mattie's age, and she'll be needing playmates soon. We could ask them over for lunch—go on a picnic or something." But except for her job at Bellawood, Melody didn't seem interested in outside activities.

Dr. Rhinehardt, Eliza's counseling professor of history, was holding a teaching assistantship for her in California, and she had to decide if she would accept it before the end of August. That would mean either renting or selling the house within the next few months. What would Melody do then?

Gradually, but surely, Melody Lamb had established herself on Habersham Street as kind of a little sister, and as much as Eliza cared for the baby, she still wasn't crazy about having responsibilities thrust upon her.

But Melody had loved Martha Figg, and that was enough. For now.

"If you didn't remember my mother so well, I wouldn't swear you're the Melody I knew," Eliza told her one night as they cleaned up after supper. Melody had made sponge cake from Martha Figg's recipe, the first she'd had since she'd lived there as a child, she said.

"How can you say that? Do you want to see my driver's license?" Melody sloshed soapy water on the floor.

"I've seen your driver's license," Eliza said. "Oh, I *know* you're Melody, it's just that you don't seem to remember a whole lot about the time you were here."

"I remember my kindergarten teacher, Mrs. Langford. I thought she was the prettiest thing! Wore purple a lot, and gave us those little candy hearts on Valentine's Day." Melody leaned against the sink and watched the water drain away. "And I remember the day I left here. I didn't want to go."

"I know. Mama cried for a week. It was awful." Eliza hung up the damp dish towel. Melody still stood at the sink, her shoulders hunched. "I have pictures of you in your Easter dress," Eliza said. "It was yellow, remember?"

Melody nodded. "I had new white sandals."

"And I think there's one made that summer. You're sitting on the back steps with Smoky, the pretty gray cat with green eyes. You loved that cat!"

Melody smiled. "Smoky, yes! Was that her name? I played with her all the time. Could I see the pictures?"

"Sure. If I can find them." Eliza turned off the kitchen light on her way out. "And while we're sharing, I'd love to see a picture of Sonny. Is that where Mattie gets her funny cowlick?"

"I have our wedding pictures put away somewhere, but I think there's a snapshot of the two of us in my stationery box. I'll look."

Eliza shuffled through photograph albums while Melody tiptoed about upstairs. The baby slept in a crib by her mother's bed, and had just begun to sleep through the night. A few minutes later Melody came downstairs and slipped two snapshots into Eliza's lap. They showed Melody and a pleasant-faced young man with short sandy hair posing arm in arm by a palm tree with the ocean in the background.

"The people at the hotel took these on our honeymoon," Melody said. "We never did get around to buying a camera." She picked up one of the pictures and examined it. "Mattie's face is shaped just like his . . . and look at me. I can't even look at his picture without starting to cry. I've got to get over this."

"You will," Eliza told her. "It just takes time." At least that's what everybody told her. She hoped they knew what they were talking about. Eliza held the photograph of Mattie's young parents in the light. There was little doubt that this man was Mattie's father. The baby even had his wide smile. So there really was a Sonny Lamb.

Eliza wished she could be as certain of Melody. Her kindergarten teacher had been Mrs. Lang, not Langford. And the Figgs had never owned a gray cat named Smoky.

CHAPTER NINE

Eliza brushed her hair from underneath, lifting the weight of it off her neck. The air was hot and humid, and even though it was early, she already felt sticky from the heat. Maybe she should have it cut short, really short in one of those voguish tapered styles, but her thick, reddish-brown hair was her best feature and Eliza knew it. She also knew it suited her trimmed just above the shoulders so that it turned under slightly on the ends. She threw down the brush, added a dab of lipstick and straightened her skirt. She hated to leave for Bellawood before Melody got back from her walk without a chance to say goodbye to Mattie, but that garden club was due from Gainesville this morning, and she was supposed to speak to them about early herb gardens and their medicinal uses. Also, it looked as if it might rain, and she'd hate to have Melody and the baby get caught in a downpour.

Downstairs in the kitchen Eliza glanced at the clock over the stove. It was shaped like a teapot and her mother had gotten it with stamps when Eliza was a little girl. It

77

had been one of the things she hadn't changed when she had the house painted back in the spring, but what a relief to get rid of that wallpaper with the vegetables on it in the breakfast room. And the new tile floor made the whole room look brighter.

Eliza poured a second cup of coffee and took it out to the porch. Maybe she would see the two of them coming around the curve at the end of the block. Melody always took the same route, turning left at the corner of Henry Grady Street and making a wide loop back home to Habersham. As far as Eliza knew, she never stopped to talk, never varied in her course, but it was after seven-thirty and Melody had planned to drop Mattie by the sitter's at eight.

Melody had been disappointed in her search for a day care facility, but during the process, somebody had recommended Mrs. Tutwiler. Beatrice Tutwiler probably wasn't as old as Eliza's mother would have been, but she had raised two sons and taught the fifth grade for over twenty years before she moved to Minerva with her husband a little over a year before, and as soon as Melody found her, she began to relax a little. When Eliza met Mrs. Tutwiler, she knew why. Mrs. Tutwiler was in control and you knew it. She also knew she would never call this woman Bea. Or Beatrice. She would always call her Mrs. Tutwiler.

This was the second week they had taken Mattie to the neat gray cottage, and the baby didn't seem to mind at all. In fact, Melody had admitted being a little disappointed that her daughter went to another so freely.

A couple of raindrops plopped on the fig bush beside the porch, and Eliza looked at her watch. It was a quarter to eight. Melody had never been this late, and Eliza felt her irritation at having to wait grow into something more: a sickening little flutter in her stomach, an ache behind the eyes. What in the world was keeping her? If she had run somewhere to get out of the rain, she would have called by now. Unless there had been an accident.

Eliza ran inside long enough to grab her car keys. Maybe Melody had found a friend, someone to talk to, and forgotten the time. She would probably find her turning the corner at the end of the street, trying to beat the rain. No harm done. After all, this soft summer shower was little more than a sprinkle. A few blots of the towel would solve everything. So why did she have this rock where her heart should be? Eliza could hear herself breathing, and her hands felt welded to the steering wheel. The streets were deserted.

She saw Lydia Stovall backing out of her driveway about halfway up the street and hurried to overtake her. Lydia owned the children's shop downtown where Eliza and Melody had shopped for the baby only a few weeks before, and Eliza hoped she would remember them.

The woman smiled and waved, then pulled over when Eliza beeped frantically on her horn. Of course she remembered Melody, and that adorable baby. And did that little yellow smock wash up okay? It was supposed to be permanent press. Lydia frowned when Eliza told her what had happened. Why no, she hadn't seen Melody and the baby, or anybody else for that matter. Her alarm hadn't worked and she was running late. Her shiny black pump tapped the gas pedal. "I'm sure she just stopped in somewhere, probably didn't even think of the time." Lydia glanced in the mirror and made a face. "My goodness, you'd think I could get lipstick on straight by now, wouldn't you?"

The rain was coming down harder as Eliza climbed back into her car. She didn't see any traffic on the short lane that connected Habersham to Henry Grady, and if anyone had been out walking, they had taken shelter. Just on the chance that Melody might have tried a new route and become lost, she turned down several side streets, but except for a sanitation truck, she didn't meet a soul. The white-clad worker (Eliza wondered why they wore white!) who emptied garbage into the truck looked at her as if she were crazy as she jumped out at him in the rain.

No, he said, shaking his head. He hadn't seen no woman with a baby.

Eliza drove slowly home, afraid to take her eyes from the road. Ordinary things engraved themselves on her mind so that she remembered them long afterward. A child's wading pool turned upside down against a tree; a bright red bike left in somebody's driveway, wheels spinning; a black lab puppy with a tennis shoe in its mouth trotting proudly across a lawn. Summer things. Innocent things.

When she turned back into Habersham Street, she didn't want to look. They'll be on the porch watching for me, she thought, wondering where I've been. Or the telephone would be ringing, and it would be Melody in her not-quite-grownup voice calling to tell her she was in somebody's kitchen having a cup of tea and not to worry.

But she wasn't. The house was empty and no one had phoned. Melody's old Honda, packed and ready with diaper bag and formula, waited in the driveway. It was after eight.

Upstairs Melody's room had that scattered look as if someone had left in a hurry. Her bed was made, but rumpled. The paisley shirtwaist dress she planned to wear to work hung primly on the closet door. Waiting.

Eliza found Mrs. Tutwiler's phone number taped to the refrigerator. Maybe the sitter had heard something, but Melody hadn't called.

"I can't imagine where she is," Eliza told her, "but I'll let you know as soon as I hear anything."

The woman was quiet for a minute. "I do hope everything's all right. I've told Melody she's taking a chance walking that baby alone as early as that. There's not many people about, and you just don't know what might happen. Why, my cousin in Memphis had a neighbor who was . . ." Mrs. Tutwiler cleared her throat. "Well I know she'll turn up soon, but you will let me know, won't you?"

Eliza sat in the old kitchen chair with the new bright

poppy print cushion. She felt weak inside, and helpless, like she had when she was seven and had gotten lost playing on the escalators in Rich's Department Store. Dorcas! Dorcas would know what to do.

"How long has she been gone?" Her neighbor came in the back way, stepping out of her wet shoes on the porch.

Eliza wanted to throw herself in her plump, motherly arms, but if she did, she knew she'd cry.

"Over an hour now. Almost an hour and a half." Eliza didn't have to look at the clock. Each second that went by was like a dripping water faucet. "I've called a couple of people who live along that route, but nobody's seen her."

Dorcas frowned. "What about Jessie? She never misses a thing."

"Jessie doesn't answer. Her garage door's closed, but she could be out somewhere." Eliza took her neighbor's dripping slicker and hung it by the door. "Want some coffee?"

"No, I want some help. Have you called the police yet? The hospital? Just in case there was an accident."

Eliza shook her head numbly. "I guess I was just waiting for somebody to tell me to do it, make me do it. Dorcas, I'm scared."

"I don't suppose she said anything?"

"About what? You mean about *leaving?* Why? Besides, she didn't have anything with her except that stroller and maybe an extra diaper or two. Where on earth would she go?"

Eliza looked out again at the street. "You don't suppose somebody *took* them?" Her hand was already on the telephone.

The hospital had no record of anyone fitting either description, Eliza was told.

"Are you sure? What about the emergency room?" But things were fairly calm there, as well—except for a three-year-old who had gotten into the Ex-Lax and a cook from

Bertha's Biscuits who dropped a big can of shortening on her foot. The woman on the switchboard seemed serenely amused by it all.

And except for a minor collision on the outskirts of town, the police hadn't had anyone call about an accident.

"Then I want to report a missing person—two missing people," Eliza said. "Maybe even a kidnapping!"

"Just a minute, I'm going to let you talk to Officer Mungo."

"Kemper Mungo?" Eliza remembered him from her sister Katherine's class. Tall, black and skinny, he had letters in basketball and track, even won a scholarship to some college down in south Georgia. She was surprised to find him still in Minerva.

Eliza had to remind him who she was, but he did remember Katherine, he said. They had worked on the high school annual together. He was quiet while she told him about Melody and the baby, so quiet she thought they might have been disconnected.

"How long did you say they've been gone?" he asked.

"Almost two hours . . . and I know what you're going to say: She's lost track of the time and is probably visiting somewhere. But she hasn't—listen, I know she hasn't. Something's happened to them! Isn't there anything you can do?"

"We'll do everything we can. Tell you what, I'll get on the radio to Oscar Watts in the patrol car and have him scout that area, see what he can find out. You did say Habersham and Henry Grady, didn't you? Maybe something will turn up."

"But what if it doesn't?" Oh, Lord, she was going to cry. She took a deep breath and swallowed.

"We'll deal with that when we come to it. Now look, I know you're worried, but it won't do any good to panic. I just can't put out an APB on them for being a couple of hours late, but if you don't hear something, say . . . by noon, that might put a different slant on things.

"Now, here's what I want you to do . . . first, better find a pencil and paper." His voice was kind, and Eliza silently thanked him for it. His patience gave her the composure she needed. For a while, anyway.

"I want you to make me a list," Kemper Mungo said. "Write down everybody this woman is friendly with, anyone she might stop to chat with, any relatives or business connections—things like that."

Eliza started jotting. "Just here in town?"

"Anywhere, especially if you think there's a possibility she could be somewhere else. And what about a job? Have you checked the place where she works?"

Bellawood! For the first time since Melody failed to return, Eliza remembered Bellawood. The Azalea Circle Garden Club was supposed to be there at ten, and she hadn't done a thing. But now, what did it matter?

"Don't worry another minute," Genevieve Ellison said. "We'll handle things from here. I'll call a few of the girls and tell them what's happened. Shoot! We'll just serve the Azaleas a box lunch."

Genevieve was in charge of the docents at the plantation, and had been doing it for so long, some of them joked that she was probably there when it was built. Eliza had butted heads with her a couple of times as both liked to have her own way, and Genevieve, being older and higher in the pecking order, usually got what she wanted. But Genevieve Ellison got things done, and Eliza knew she could count on her.

"Didn't see Melody's car out front; she's usually here by now. I wondered if the baby was sick or something," Genevieve said. "This really isn't like her at all . . . but I'm sure there must be a logical explanation. Try not to worry, Eliza—and do let us know, won't you?" But as skilled as she was at running things, Genevieve was no actress. She couldn't keep the anxiety from her voice.

With the kitchen table between them, Eliza and Dorcas listed everyone they could think of who had even spoken to Melody. Even so, it was a short list. A few people called wanting to know if they'd heard anything, and Eliza kept the conversation short—just in case Melody did try to get in touch. It didn't take long for word to get around in Minerva.

She wasn't surprised when a few minutes later Sydney pulled up in the driveway and ran inside with her three year old in tow. "I was downtown," she said, "and Lydia Stovall said you were out looking for Melody. When I called out at Bellawood, Genevieve gave me the news." Suddenly Syd grabbed her in an uncustomary bear hug. "Oh, God, Eliza! What can I do?"

Dorcas gave her the finished list. "Look at this," she said. "And see if you can think of anyone we've missed."

"You forgot about the man," Sydney said in a husky whisper. Her eyes had that "I don't want to have to tell you this" expression.

"What man?" Eliza said.

"The man she was afraid of. The man in the black car."

CHAPTER TEN

Kemper Mungo folded himself mantis-style in Eliza's kitchen chair and looked at the list of names. "This Mrs. Tutwiler . . . say you talked with her?"

Eliza nodded, rubbing her hands across hot marble eyes that burned even when she closed them. "Twice," she said. "I called her back a little while ago—just to be sure. She hasn't heard anything."

The tall policeman scribbled on his big yellow notepad. "Just the same, I'll have Oscar go by there. Can't hurt.

"Now, what's this about a black car? Is that for real, or some kind of boogie man—you know, like Gunny Sack Sam?"

Eliza had almost forgotten about Gunny Sack Sam, the imaginary, but none-the-less horrifying threat of retribution waiting in the shadows and around every corner for disobedient children.

Amber Gillis, who had shared a table with Eliza in kindergarten, had warned her about him in such great detail Eliza had nightmares for months.

"Melody thinks he's real—not Gunny Sack Sam, the guy in the big car," she told him. "Baxter Phillips said somebody in a black Chrysler was asking about Melody at Bellawood back when she first came here, and we did see a car like that in the parking lot when we went to her apartment."

He frowned. "We?"

"Syd and I." It had stopped raining, and Sydney stood by the window watching Jonathan racing around the Figg's backyard. "We tried to keep it in sight, see if he followed us to The Three Pigs—that barbecue place in Kennesaw, but he never showed up," Eliza said.

"Not that we know of, anyway." Sydney said.

Eliza looked at the clock. It was only a few minutes after ten, but she felt as if she had been sitting in this kitchen since time began. Dorcas had left with Baxter Phillips about an hour ago to see if they could find anyone who had seen a young woman pushing a baby in a stroller. And Syd had called the nursing home in Marietta where Melody's mother existed to see if the two of them had turned up there. They hadn't. Eliza had visited there a few times with Melody, and twice they had even taken Mattie to see her Grandmother Sutherland, but the woman didn't respond. Each time Melody would come home silent and sad, yet she kept going back. The last few times, though, Melody left the baby with Eliza.

"You say she was wearing plaid shorts? Pink and purple. You're sure about the color?" Kemper Mungo looked up at Eliza as she walked again to the window.

"I'm sure. She had on a T-shirt too, I think, under that baggy blue cotton shirt. It was one of her husband's; she liked to walk in it. And a big straw hat with a flowered band around it. Melody's careful about her complexion. Burns easily."

He nodded. "And the baby?"

The baby. She didn't know. Mattie had so many clothes. A diaper, of course, and some kind of light shirt or dress. Clean and dainty. Melody always dressed her nicely. Eliza shook her head.

"There is an off chance," Kemper said, "that she got in the car with somebody. Someone she knew. Trusted. A friend, maybe."

"Melody doesn't have many friends," Eliza told him. "Nobody close. And she would never get in a car with a stranger. Never."

"Especially somebody in a big black car," Syd said.

The policeman looked down at his hands, bounced the pencil a few times on the pad. "Not willingly, anyway," he said. He didn't say it to anybody in particular. He just said it.

"But what about the stroller?" Eliza said. "We would have seen it if she had just left it somewhere beside the road, and it would take a few minutes to lift it into a car. You'd think somebody would have noticed it."

"And maybe they did." The policeman stood. "Look, I know it doesn't seem this way to you, but it's still early yet. You said yourself she'd been acting kind of peculiar. She might have gone for a long walk—just to be alone for a while, to think."

"In the rain, with a baby?" Eliza turned to face him. "You really don't believe that, do you?" She looked at Syd. Syd the mother. "At least she had a few extra diapers, and I saw her take along a bottle of juice in case Mattie got fussy.

"The baby's breast fed," Eliza explained. "Melody always fed her when she got back from her walk, before she left for Bellawood."

"Oh, dear Lord! Jonathan, come here!" Syd ushered in a mud-streaked toddler clutching a fistful of pinks—roots and all. Dirt fell to the floor in clumps and she quickly scooped it up with a wet paper towel. "Sorry, Eliza. We're in the way, I know. Better get this one home." Syd rinsed the child's hands at the sink.

"No, you're not! I'm glad you're here—both of you." Eliza rescued the damaged flowers and gave them back to Jonathan who had started to cry. "He's probably thirsty. Want some juice, Jonathan?"

Kemper stood in front of the refrigerator, and Eliza noticed he was tall enough to see the dust on top. Most people weren't. Over the policeman's shoulder, Eliza could see an appointment card held to the refrigerator with a magnet that looked like a chocolate chip cookie. Melody had put it there so she wouldn't forget Mattie's next scheduled visit to the pediatrician. The baby's stuffed pink bunny—the one that played "Peter Cottontail," sat on the counter next to a box of Gerber's oatmeal. Her little dish with the Three Bears on the bottom, that once belonged to Eliza, waited next to the stove.

Kemper moved aside for her to open the refrigerator, smiling slightly and shaking his head.

"What is it?" Eliza asked.

"Nothing. I'm just kind of surprised to find you here doing ordinary things like everybody else. Thought you'd be off climbing the Matterhorn or something."

"It couldn't be any rougher than this," Eliza said.

A few minutes after Sydney left, Dorcas and Baxter trailed in to say that except for the Fossetts' fourteen-year-old son who had been forced (according to him) to weed the flower border, no one had seen Melody and her baby since she left the house that morning. The Fossetts lived about a block and half away on Habersham, Baxter pointed out; which meant that whoever took Melody and her baby (and it was beginning to look as if that was what had happened), must have come along soon after she turned the corner.

"The Fossett boy—he didn't hear or see anything different?" Kemper asked, taking long strides to the back door.

Dorcas shook her head and reached for Eliza's hand. "Just the dog—the Thornbroughs' dog, The Boss, barking like crazy. But he always does that." She frowned as he let the screen door slam. "Where are you going now?"

Kemper yelled over his shoulder. "To the car. I'm putting an APB out on those two! I think we've waited long
enough."

He paused for a second at the bottom of the steps.
"Did either of you happen to see Jessie Gilreath while
you were out looking around?"

Dorcas folded her hefty arms and peered from beneath
her brows in the vague direction of her neighbor's house.
"That Jessie! Surprised she hadn't been over here yet with
one of those sickening sweet pies. She must've noticed
something's going on."

"Didn't show up at Bellawood this morning, either,"
Kemper Mungo said. "Last time I checked out there, that
lady who kind of runs things—you know, Mrs. Ellison,
said they'd been trying to call. It's her day to work in the
gift shop, she said. Not like her to forget like that."

"Tell me about it!" Dorcas rolled her eyes. "Jessie'd
rather put on that old green polka-dotted dress and that
silly little cap and pretend she's Bella Pitts than have tea
and dainties at the White House. And you know how that
outfit makes her look bilious," she whispered aside to
Eliza. "And skinnier than a pole bean!"

"Uh—don't you mean bean pole?" Baxter said.

"Whatever," Dorcas said.

Baxter kind of shuffled around in the kitchen doorway,
and if he'd had a hat in his hands, he would have turned
it. "Can I get you anything?" he said, following Eliza with
pleading blue eyes.

*Yes, damn it! Go back out there and find them! Bring
them both here within five minutes . . . I'm timing you!*
Eliza wanted to scream at him, but she managed a rea-
sonably calm reply, thanking him for his efforts. How
could he possibly know how much she was hurting?
How could anyone? Eliza knew he was in a hurry to be
away. She didn't blame him.

Eliza stood in the upstairs hallway and looked out at
the summer morning street. Two skinny girls raced by on

bikes, and a third, chunkier one pedaled after them, all
red faced and bent over. The Boss hated bikers, but she
didn't hear him bark. Too tired, probably, or too hot. A
car passed. Two cars. Three. Downstairs, Dorcas ran water into the sink, then bumped the kitchen chairs about to
sweep under the table. Food was already coming in. Tuna
salad, peach cobbler, and something gooey and green in
a glass dish. Eliza didn't want to think about eating.

She straightened the spread on Melody's bed and hung
her blue cotton dress in the closet. A folded crib sheet
waited to be put on the baby's mattress, and she tucked it
carefully in place, then plopped a droopy-eared Piglet at
the head, glad of something to do.

A car door slammed, and Eliza heard her father's voice
in the hall. It was the same voice that had soothed
skinned knees, told bedtime stories, calmed piano recital
jitters. The voice that always made things right. Until last
year.

Crying, Eliza ran downstairs to meet him.

He held her, stroked her hair and made those familiar
noises—not words exactly, but some kind of mumbled
formula for setting the world back on its course. But he
seemed different, thinner. She could feel his ribs beneath
his clothes.

"How long has she been gone?" Ben Figg asked, leading his daughter into the living room where they sat, still
holding hands. "Have the police been here?"

"Kemper Mungo just left—you remember him—gradu-
ated with Katherine," Eliza said. "He's already put out an
APB. They usually wait twenty-four hours, but in this case
. . . well . . . they've been missing since early morning." Eliza wiped her nose with the clump of tissues she
had been absentmindedly carrying around. "I gave him
Melody's wedding picture and one of those we had made
of Mattie last month at Sears. You know, the one where
her eyes look so big?" Eliza would never admit how
many prints she had ordered—not that she meant to actually carry them around, or anything like that. "I don't

know what else to do! What could've happened to them?''

He squeezed her hand. "I don't know, Honey. That's what I want to find out.''

Eliza noticed he didn't promise anything.

She was forewarned of Olivia's presence when she heard voices in the kitchen, and her father's new bride followed Dorcas into the room, looking trim and cool in her jade blazer and white pleated skirt. Standing there beside their neighbor, who wore at least a size sixteen, Olivia appeared almost undernourished, Eliza thought.

And for the first time that day she took a full look at her father. Ben Figg was a thinner, fitter image of the man she knew. His face, lightly tanned, seemed firmer, and that bulge around his midriff was gone. Why, he looked almost young!

It made her aware of how long it had been since she'd seen him. The two of them talked frequently over the phone, but except for a few visits back in the winter, their attempts to socialize as a family had fizzled into something between a blind date and a trip to the periodontist.

Ben Figg jumped up and gave Dorcas an affectionate kiss on the cheek. "What's that I smell?" He followed his nose into the kitchen. "Chocolate! I knew it!" He ran the tip of his finger around the icing on a cake that sat on the counter, then licked it off as if he hadn't had anything to eat since yesterday. "Umm! You make this, Dorcas?"

"No. Frances Reece brought it over, but I'll sure cut you a hunk. Sit down." Dorcas snatched a plate from the cabinet.

Ben Figg glanced at his wife. "Uh— better not." He opened the refrigerator. "What's this? Tuna salad? Looks good." He lifted the plastic wrap to get a better look.

"My God, Daddy! What's wrong with you? How can

you even think about food?" Eliza clamped a hand over her mouth.

"Sorry, Honey, but it's been several hours since I ate. I don't function too well on an empty stomach."

"From the looks of you, it's been longer than several hours. When's the last time you had a decent meal? You've lost an awful lot of weight." Eliza didn't look at Olivia who twittered about like a little wren dressed in parakeet's plumage, but she glimpsed her out of the corner of her eye.

"I try to see he eats healthy," Olivia said, rustling about with a grocery sack. "His blood pressure's much too high, and his cholesterol . . . here, I brought some disposable plates. You must be hungry, too—all of you." Olivia dealt them out on the table. "Why don't we all sit down. I expect we'll be able to think better with a little something in our stomachs."

"Suit yourself!" Eliza turned away. "Somehow, I just don't feel like a picnic today.

"And you!" She whirled to face her father. "Just this once, couldn't you have come by yourself? This isn't the time for an experiment in domestic relations."

She knew she had gone too far before she had the words out, but it was like trying to staunch a geyser. Eliza saw the hurt in Ben Figg's eyes, the shock and disapproval in Dorcas's. And Olivia. Well, Olivia just kind of disappeared behind the refrigerator door and began snatching things out and practically pitching them onto the table.

Dorcas took her hand. Firmly. "Let's go upstairs," she said. "See if you can't lie down for a while, close your eyes."

Eliza didn't want to go upstairs and lie down, but she didn't know what else to do. She followed her neighbor through the sitting room with its bright new curtains and into the hall, fresh with paint and wallpaper. Melody had helped her decide on the pattern of billowing ferns and wild flowers, and it looked like a blurred mural.

Neither Dorcas nor Eliza spoke. The world was mean today, and Eliza felt mean too.

She was halfway up the stairs when Kemper Mungo came by to tell them they had found Melody's hat and shirt beside the river.

CHAPTER ELEVEN

"Where?" Eliza said. "Take me there! I want to see."

Kemper Mungo took her by the shoulders and gently forced her into a chair. "It wouldn't do any good," he said. "We have people out there now searching along the banks, the whole area. You'll do better to stay here."

"But Mattie . . ." Eliza tugged at his arm. "Was there any sign of the baby?"

The policeman shook his head solemnly. "No, just the blue cotton work shirt you said Melody was wearing, some pink canvas flats, and that big straw hat." He hesitated, glancing at Ben as if for reassurance. "I hate to ask this of you, but I'll need you to look at them."

Eliza nodded, and for the first time she noticed the large plastic bag he had left just inside the door. There was no mistaking the hat with the bright pink and green flowered band. The shoes were new. Melody had bought them on sale the week before. "Where?" she asked. "Where by the river?"

"Just below the bridge—the one on Damascus Church Road, about a mile outside the city limits. Some berry pickers found them lying on those big rocks there—right in sight of the road."

Ben Figg sat with his head bowed; clasped hands dangled between his knees. "Well now," he said, looking up. "Maybe she just went in to cool off. It must be ninety degrees out there, and that's a popular picnic spot. Been there myself."

Eliza could look at her father and tell he didn't believe that fairy tale himself, but Kemper Mungo nodded. "That's what the woman who found them thought at first. They were there when she and her boys started down that little side path to pick blackberries before it got so hot. When she saw they were still there over an hour later, she thought she'd better report it."

Dorcas stood by Eliza's chair with her hand resting warm and heavy on her shoulder. "Why, that must be four or five miles from here," she said. "Melody wouldn't have walked out there in this heat."

"She wouldn't have taken Mattie there either, not alone." Eliza said. "Melody would never hurt that baby!" Eliza reached for Dorcas's hand. "But what was she doing there?"

"She must have left Mattie somewhere," Dorcas said. "Somewhere safe. But where?"

"She has to be between here and the river," Eliza said. "Melody wouldn't have had time to go very far . . . Unless somebody has taken her!" She jumped to her feet and grabbed the purse she had slung on the sofa earlier. The beige straw bag looked foreign to her. It belonged to that other Eliza.

Ben Figg reached out to stop her. "Wait a minute, here! Where are you going?"

She shoved his hand aside. "Somebody could have taken Mattie! Don't you see that's what happened? They left Melody at the river and kidnapped the baby." Eliza shook the bag and heard the rattle of keys inside. "I can't just sit here—I've got to find her!"

"And how do you propose to do that?" Dorcas said. "Go door to door?"

"If I have to. At least it's something." Eliza looked up to find Kemper Mungo standing in front of her. "Get out of my way, Kemper, I mean it!" A cold calmness came over her. She felt like a walking cannon. Eliza had promised Melody she would take care of Mattie, and it was up to her to find her.

"I know how you feel," the policeman said. "But right now is not the time for you to go driving around. You don't belong behind the wheel of a car. Let us handle it. Please."

"I'll drive her, Officer." Dorcas took the handbag from her, and Eliza noticed the look that passed between them. *Just humor her, I'll see that she doesn't hurt anyone.* She didn't care what they thought as long as she could get out of this house.

"I'll ride along with you," Ben said. "We'll all look."

Olivia spoke from behind them. "Then I'll stay here. Somebody should be here to answer the phone, and I imagine you'll want iced tea." She folded a red plaid dish towel as she talked, and Eliza noticed she had shed the green blazer. She had almost forgotten she was there.

Kemper stepped back and spoke softly to Dorcas as she passed. "Stay away from the river."

Eliza knew he hadn't meant for her to hear, but she had, and the words had gone home. "They're dragging it, aren't they?"

He tried to smile. "No, of course not. Too soon for that."

"Then divers. You're using divers." Eliza felt her father's hand on her arm, but she had to ask. "You haven't found the stroller? Mattie's stroller? Surely you don't think the baby is—"

Kemper shook his head. "Eliza, there was no indication of the baby being there. If we'd found the stroller— anything—I'd tell you."

"What time is it?" Eliza asked. Since Dorcas didn't have her car keys, she drove Eliza's red Dodge, and it seemed to take her an eternity to back out of the drive- way.

Dorcas pointed to the clock on the dashboard. Eliza had forgotten the damned thing even had a clock. It was almost a quarter after one. Melody and the baby had been gone over six hours.

"Let's stop by the Fossetts'," Eliza said. "That Fossett boy was the last one to see them. Maybe he'll remember something else."

Dorcas slowed, but didn't stop as they neared the neat brick ranch house. "The police have already been there," she said. "Besides, Randy Fossett said his mother called him to breakfast right after he saw them pass, and he didn't go back outside for almost an hour."

Ben Figg leaned forward from the backseat. "I suppose they've searched her car?"

"Diaper bag was packed," Eliza told him. "Formula, diapers, extra clothes. Melody wasn't going anywhere— except to Mrs. Tutwiler's and Bellawood."

The streets sizzled in the sun; things looked hazy, blurry, like they do in a mirage in the movies. Maybe she would see Melody standing there ahead of them in a shimmering vapor, and she would vanish with a poof when they got close. Melody would be the type to do that. But Mattie? Not Mattie!

Mattie would be hungry. She would be wet and hot. Furious! Mattie would cry. Good! Eliza hoped she would scream loud and long. She bit her lip picturing the baby abandoned along the side of the road in tall weeds, un- protected from sun and insects. Or she could be in a car with strangers, awful strangers, speeding toward who- knows-where.

Eliza turned to Dorcas who sat as straight as her round

figure would allow. Now and then she took off her bifo-
cals and wiped the moisture on her sleeve. "Dorcas?"
Eliza ran a finger through the dust on the dashboard.

"What, Honey?"

"Do you think Melody had time to feed her before she
. . . did whatever it was she did?"

Dorcas slowed to avoid a cat that ran in front of the
car. "I don't know . . . but yes, I think she probably
did."

"Let's try that back way that comes out on the east side
of town, down past where the old cannery used to be,"
Ben said after they had covered the same area several
times. Houses were shabbier in this part of town. Grass
grew high, unencumbered by rusting machinery, old
tires, furniture with exposed innards. They drove past a
small industrial section: fertilizer plant, feed mill, plumb-
ing supply, but no abandoned baby and no pedestrian in
sight to question.

"Guess everybody's inside where it's cool," Ben said.

The faded buildings, straggly bushes, crumbling as-
phalt road smeared together as Eliza strained her eyes,
leaning over the dashboard, to see what she hoped, yet
dreaded to find. "There must be a way to go about this,"
she said. "I just wish I knew what it was. Maybe we'd
better see what's happened at home." It would take
about ten minutes to drive back to Habersham Street. Ten
minutes to hope.

A block from home Eliza saw someone standing in the
front yard waving. Someone tall. Sydney. She ran toward
them as they turned into the driveway, and was joined by
Olivia who came flying down the steps.

Sydney didn't wait for Eliza to open the door, but
reached through the open car window and grabbed her
around the neck. "They've found the baby and she's fine!
Kemper just left—said he'd meet us there."

If Syd weren't holding her down, Eliza felt she might
float right out the window. She had never experienced

such lightness; it was like drinking hot mulled wine on an empty stomach. It was not until after all the hugging and crying that she remembered to ask where Mattie was.

"Willie Westbrook found her on the porch of that little chapel behind the Episcopal Church," Sydney said.

"Willie's sexton over there," she explained to Olivia. "About half a bubble off plumb, but he's been there forever. Real persnickety too; better not let him see you litter his grounds."

"What about Melody?" Eliza felt guilty for not asking sooner.

"Nothing yet, as far as we know," Olivia told her. "They've got Mattie at the parish house; the minister's wife's taking care of her."

"She's probably starving and mad as a wet hornet," Eliza said. "I'd better grab a bottle." Melody was gradually weaning the baby, but kept extra breast milk in the refrigerator.

Melody. If Melody meant to abandon her baby, why didn't she leave her with Eliza instead of in front of a church? And the Episcopal Church at that. They didn't even belong there. It didn't make sense!

"I don't understand what took them so long to find her," Ben said, making room for his wife and Syd in the backseat. "Has she been sitting out there in that stroller all this time?"

"The church office is closed on Friday," Syd told him. "Nobody was around but Willie. Kemper said he found the baby's shoes first—one out by the front steps, and the other on that brick walk to the chapel. Couldn't understand why somebody would go and mess up his yard that way."

Eliza looked back at Syd. "Melody must have put them there, hoping somebody would get curious."

"Well, Willie wasn't so much curious as he was put out," Syd said. "But he did find the baby. She was asleep in her stroller just to one side of the chapel door. He said it looked like somebody had parked her there in the shade—it had stopped raining by then—and gone inside to pray, or maybe to meet with the minister about something. Sometimes people like to do that, he says, because the chapel's small. They feel comfortable there. That must have been about ten."

"You mean he just left her?" Dorcas said. "Left her out there wet and hungry in that stroller?"

Sydney shrugged. "She didn't look wet and hungry to Willie. She just looked asleep. It wasn't until about an hour later when he was spraying those azaleas out front that he heard her crying. He'd just plain forgotten about her, Willie told Kemper, and he couldn't find anybody to tell him what to do . . . so he picked her up and carried her around with him for a while. He discovered the bottle of apple juice and gave her that when he couldn't find her mama. Then he just waited around for the Merediths to get home."

"The Merediths? The minister's family, I guess." Olivia looked at her husband as she spoke.

Sydney nodded. "He was making hospital visits, and his wife was teaching a summer school class. Said she drove up about a quarter till one and found Willie in the porch swing singing to the baby."

"It does look like he would've called somebody," Dorcas said as they turned down a wide shady street.

"Willie can't read," Syd said. "I guess he would've called nine eleven if he thought it was an emergency, but the baby wasn't sick or hurt or anything. I suppose he thought her mother just forgot about her."

Eliza saw the square brown steeple reaching through the trees in the next block. The Episcopal Church was built of stone the color of gingerbread, and was screened from its neighbors on either side by a small wooded area. Eliza's mother had called it "The Little Brown Church in the Wildwood." She thought of that now as they stopped in front of the parish house next door. Could Martha Figg have prevented Melody from doing what she did?

A familiar police car was parked in the driveway, and

Kemper Mungo waved to them from the porch. Eliza threw open her door and raced toward him across the lawn. Behind him Doris Meredith stood with Mattie in her arms. She smiled down at the baby, but her face was solemn when she greeted Eliza.

Kemper waited until she held, kissed and cried over Mattie before he led her aside. "Melody left a note with the baby," he said.

"A note? What did she say? Kemper, tell me—what kind of note? Oh, God! Was it suicide?"

"Well, that's what we're supposed to believe," he said. "But now I'm not so sure. We found blood on the baby's blanket, and as far as we can tell, it didn't come from Mattie."

CHAPTER TWELVE

"What do you mean, *as far as you can tell?* Mattie's not hurt? She's not bleeding, is she?" Eliza looked at the baby happily reaching for Dorcas's glasses as the two sat on the Meredith's sofa. She *seemed* fine, but you never knew, and Eliza had heard about such awful things happening—things she didn't even want to think about.

Eliza grabbed Kemper's arm. Her legs felt as if they had no bones in them at all. "Has a doctor seen her? I'll call Dr. Satterlee!"

Kemper Mungo sighed and shook his head. "That's already taken care of. He's on his way, but Mattie's fine, Eliza. Really. Mrs. Meredith bathed her, changed her. One of our officers, Bonnie Thomas, bought formula from the drugstore . . . see—she's full and happy." He followed her with a worried face as she went to the front door to look for the doctor.

"What about the blanket?" Eliza asked. "Where is it?"

"We took it in for testing. Found it jammed beneath the baby's clothes in the stroller."

"Was there much blood?" The thought of blood on a baby's blanket made Eliza sick. It had better not be Mattie's!

"Only a smear; couldn't be more than a few drops." Kemper frowned. "I don't suppose you know the mother's blood type?"

"Melody? Yes, she was O negative. I know because she told me her husband was positive and they had to worry about the baby being jaundiced. She said they checked her blood a lot when she was pregnant just to be sure everything was all right."

"And was it?"

"Yes, they say with the first one it usually is, but they have to take precautions. Mattie's positive like her father, but I don't remember the type."

"Another thing," the policeman said. "I'll need a sample of Melody's handwriting. I meant to ask your father to bring one."

"He probably wouldn't know where to look." Eliza remembered the straw handbag she had thrown on the Meredith's porch. "I might have something right here—a grocery list Melody gave me last night. Would that do?"

"It's a start," he said when Eliza gave him the square of lavender paper. Ingredients for what she intended to be Saturday's dinner were written with purple ink in Melody's small slanted writing. Sydney and her husband were to have joined them for shrimp creole and peach shortcake.

Was it Melody's blood on the blanket? Eliza's head ached from holding back tears. Now she felt them welling behind her eyes, rolling silently down her face, and searched in her bag for a tissue. Poor, scared Melody! "Could I see the note? What did it say?" She couldn't believe Melody would do such a thing—not since she had Mattie!

Kemper Mungo brought out a folded page from a composition book. It had a jagged tear across the bottom as if it had been ripped out in a hurry. In a handwriting similar to Melody's, someone had used a black ballpoint to write:

> *Please take care of my little girl.*
> *I just can't go on living without*
> *Sonny. I hope you will forgive me.*
>   *Melody Lamb*

"Short and sweet," Kemper said as Eliza stared at the paper. "Well, what do you think?"

"It looks like Melody's writing, but I couldn't say for sure. She doesn't use paper like this, and I don't think she even has a black pen." Eliza gave him back the note. "If Melody did . . . well . . . do what this note says, why didn't she just leave Mattie with me? Why would she pack a diaper bag for the sitter and then walk the baby all the way to the Episcopal Church?"

Eliza looked up to see her father standing in the hallway behind her. "It must be three miles from here to that river, and it's the hottest day we've had all summer. If Melody was going to jump in the river, you'd think she'd at least drive herself there," she said.

Ben Figg nodded. "I agree, it doesn't make sense, but then someone desperate enough to commit suicide doesn't think rationally. I just don't understand why Melody would do this! It isn't like her."

And how would you know? Eliza thought. Her father had seen Melody two or three times at the most since she came back to Minerva to live. His face looked drawn, and his eyes were weak and red. Eliza recognized the signs. He was going to cry and she would have to comfort him as she had when her mother died. And who would comfort her?

Eliza pretended she didn't see her father's outstretched hand, and when she saw Dr. Satterlee striding up the front walk, hurried out to meet him. The doctor couldn't have arrived at a better time.

The baby was fine, he said. Not a mark on her except for a mosquito bite that had been there before. Eliza looked her over several times during the night just to make sure. She had spent the night in Melody's bed so she could be near the baby. Mattie had slept without waking—which is more than you could say for Eliza, who dozed off periodically only to wake with a heavy awareness of where she was, and why. And each time the memory of what had happened caused increasing pain. Had Melody been trying to tell her something? Maybe she hadn't been listening.

Eliza tried to reconstruct her last conversation with Melody the night before she disappeared. They had talked about Saturday's dinner, laughed over Mattie's delight at seeing the kitten next door. Melody was thinking about getting her hair cut, she said; and did Eliza think she was too fat to wear a bikini?

Eliza had laughed outright. *"Fat?* I'll give you fat, Melody Lamb! If you swallowed an olive, you'd look pregnant."

Melody smiled and patted her stomach. She was vain about her figure. "You don't think I pooch out just a little from carrying Mattie?" There was a suit she'd seen in the mall, she said. Hot pink, but they wanted too much for it. She would wait until it went on sale, Melody decided.

Wait. Would someone who contemplated suicide show interest in changing her hairstyle? Look forward to buying a pink bikini? Eliza got out of bed when she heard the thud of the newspaper on the porch. She looked at the sleeping baby in the caressing grayness of a summer dawn, and knew as surely as she was standing there that Melody Lamb didn't take her own life.

Then where was she? Searchers had covered both sides of the river for several miles. Divers had plumbed its depths, but there was no sign of Melody Lamb—only her outer clothing left neatly on the rocks. A little too neatly,

Kemper Mungo seemed to think, and conveniently in sight of passersby. Also, Dorcas had pointed out, why would you bother to remove your shoes and shirt if you planned to drown yourself? Was she reluctant to get them wet? To ruin a new pair of shoes?

Eliza found that someone had already made coffee when she went down to the kitchen. Ben Figg stood on the back porch staring across the silent yard with a steaming mug in his hand. Eliza poured a cup and went to stand beside him. "Have you heard anything?" Her voice came out in a hushed croak.

He shook his head. "Not yet."

"Where's Olivia?"

"Left just a little while ago. She'll be back in a day or two." He took a sip of coffee. He didn't look at her. "Thought I'd walk down to the police station in a little while. See if they've learned anything new."

And get out of this house, Eliza thought. Well, she didn't blame him. "What about your frame shop?" she asked.

"Livvy can take care of it. I'm here as long as you need me, Eliza."

"I know." She almost touched his hand, but not quite. Eliza drew in her breath. "Look, I'm sorry for what I said yesterday. I was horrible, I know . . . but I didn't mean it."

He turned then and looked at her. "Yes, you were horrible; and yes, Eliza, you did mean it. I know you were scared and worried about Melody and the baby, but it wasn't Olivia's fault. You're apologizing to the wrong person, you know."

"I know." Eliza had meant to say something to Olivia that morning . . . or maybe that afternoon . . . well, the next day for sure. She was still trying to deal with a strange woman sleeping with her father in her parents' bedroom. "Olivia must've left while I was in the shower," she told him. "If you talk with her today, I wish you'd tell her what I said."

Ben Figg shook his head and looked at her with his sad face, just as he had when he learned she'd lied about dating Chris Wylie when she was eighteen. Her parents hated Chris Wylie almost as much as they hated musicians who grabbed their private parts in public, or desecrated the American flag. "No, that's something you'll have to do yourself, Eliza."

Later, after her father left for town, Eliza took Mattie out on the front porch and sat in the swing to give her a bottle. Was it only yesterday she had waited here expecting Melody to appear at the end of the street? Eliza had a strange feeling that if she sat in the same place today, it would give Melody another chance.

She was sitting there when Sydney drove up and joined her. "Any news?" The swing jounced as Syd sat beside her.

"I talked with Kemper a few minutes ago," Eliza said. "They put out an APB to every police station within a hundred miles of here, but they haven't heard a thing."

"What about the black car?"

"You mean the Chrysler Baxter saw? Well, Kemper knows about it. Said they were keeping an eye out for it —or one that looks like that. We didn't have a license number to give him." Eliza put the baby on her shoulder. "I'm afraid if there was a black car, it would have been long gone by the time the police got involved." She jumped as the telephone rang inside.

"Stay right here, I'll get it." Syd put a hand on her shoulder. "Eddie has the kids, so I'm here for the morning, or until he flees the country—whichever comes first."

"Who was it?" Eliza could read Syd's face well enough to know the call had not been about Melody.

"Lydia Stovall. Wanted to know if you've heard anything. If she could help."

"She's the fifth person who's called this morning; two were reporters," Eliza said. "It's in today's paper; did you see? I've already told them all I can. I can't believe this is happening!" Mattie began to fuss, and Eliza settled her in her little infant swing on the shady end of the porch. "I wonder if she misses her mother yet. Do you think she knows something's wrong?"

"Who knows what babies think? I'm sure she must be aware that an important part of her life is missing."

"Oh, God! I'm not doing a very good job of this. I wish Melody would come back! Where could she be, Syd? Don't you wish we could live yesterday over again? I'd never let them out of my sight!"

"Eliza, come on now, it isn't your fault." Sydney put an arm about her shoulders. "Go on and cry if you want to. It's all right to cry. It's just Mattie and me, and we don't care—do we, Mattie?"

"Not anymore." Eliza wiped her eyes on the diaper she had slung over her shoulder. "Isn't that Penny Shillinglaw headed this way?"

"Going to feed that dog, I guess, or out on the prowl for boys. She won't even notice us here."

But this time Penny wasn't wearing earphones or jogging at her usual pace. She turned in the Figgs' front walk and stepped hesitantly up to the porch. When Penny saw the baby, Eliza thought the girl was going to cry. "Oh, Mattie! I'm so glad you're all right!" Penny got down on her knees to hug the baby who smiled and held out her arms. "She is all right, isn't she?"

"She's fine, Penny, thank you." Eliza was touched, and a little surprised to see Penny show concern—even affection, for Mattie.

"What about Melody? Have you heard what happened? I hope she's going to be okay."

"I hope so too," Eliza said. "But we haven't heard anything yet. By the way, you weren't out walking yesterday morning, were you? We're trying to find anybody who might have seen Melody or noticed anything unusual."

Penny jumped to her feet and backed into the fern

stand. "I wasn't even here yesterday morning! Had to go to the dentist."

What was wrong with the girl? She acted as though Eliza might go for her fingernails with bamboo slivers. "It's okay," Eliza said. "I just thought you might have been in the area, that's all."

"Why me? I live three blocks over." Penny jerked her head in the other direction and started down the steps.

Sydney raised her brows at Eliza. "But you feed the Thornbroughs' dog, don't you?" she called after her. "Aren't they out of town?"

The girl turned and frowned, shading her eyes from the sun. "Yeah, I did, but usually not until afternoon. Besides, didn't you hear? The Boss got killed yesterday morning— run over by a garbage truck."

Eliza stood and picked up Mattie as Penny hurried away. So The Boss was dead! Just wait until she told Melody! And then she remembered. "It's getting too hot out here. Let's go inside." She wondered if the Thornbroughs knew about their dog getting killed, or even if they'd care. And aside from Penny's peculiar reaction, there was something she said that bothered her. Something important.

The phone rang again, and Sydney ran to answer it. "Poor old dog!" she said over her shoulder. "Can't say I'll miss him, but I hate for him to go like that. Wonder how he got out?"

Eliza wondered too. That mysterious thing that was bothering her almost came to the surface—or it would have if somebody hadn't started screaming across the street.

CHAPTER THIRTEEN

Instinctively, Eliza wrapped both arms around Mattie and clutched her closer. Through the sitting room window she saw Lily Rose Jenkins, who "did" for Jessie Gilreath, dashing across the road and up Dorcas Young-blood's front walk, shrieking like a clarinet with a broken reed. Lily Rose must have weighed close to 250 pounds, and was sixty-five if she was a day. Eliza couldn't believe the woman could run that fast.

"What in the devil is that all about?" Syd hurried to answer the shrilling telephone. "Yes?" she yelled into the receiver. "Well, I don't know, but something's going on out there right now. A chain saw doesn't make that much noise. Screaming. Right, somebody's screaming . . . don't know . . ."

She shrugged. "Hung up."

Eliza stood by the window looking at the deserted street. The hysterical maid had disappeared inside the house next door. "Who was it?" she asked.

"Your dad; wanted to know if we'd heard anything—if

111

you were all right." She smiled. "Guess he'll be along soon now.

"What was all that yelling? What happened?"

"Lily Rose—you know, comes in Saturdays for Jessie? Covered about seventy-five yards in five seconds flat. Something must've scared the daylights out of her."

"Maybe she got a look at Jessie before she put on her makeup." Sydney staked out the other window. "Where'd she go?"

"Lily Rose? Inside with Dorcas. Damn! What's going on here?" Eliza started for the phone.

"No, wait! I hear a siren . . . it's an ambulance! Uh-oh—police too, and here comes Dorcas with Lily Rose." Sydney let the curtain fall back into place. "Come on! Let's go see what's going on."

Lily Rose planted herself like a sturdy oak in the middle of the sidewalk outside Jessie Gilreath's house and wailed. "Oh, sweet Jesus, she's in there!" She pointed wildly over her shoulder and paused to work up another good shriek. "Up yonder in the bathtub! I ain't goin' back in there—ugh-uh—no-sireee! Done seen too much already!"

Two members of the town's rescue squad had already found the unlocked side door and disappeared inside Jessie's house. A woman about Eliza's age dressed in the light blue uniform of the Minerva Police alternately mopped her red face and jotted down notes as they stood in the midmorning sun.

She had come at the usual time, the maid told her, at a little after nine, and let herself in with a key Jessie kept under a loose brick in the bottom step.

"I hollered like I always do to let her know I was there," Lily Rose said, blotting her face with a large flowered handkerchief. "Usually she's downstairs to meet me with a big old list of all them things she wants done—but not this time . . . and I knowed her car was there cause I seen it through the window of the garage.

"Oh blessed Lord!" The woman shuddered. "And

that's when I went upstairs and found her. That hall window was open—you know, the one that faces the street, and some of them red flowers was scattered on the floor. First I thought maybe she'd leaned over too far—fallen out, but the windowsill's too high for that. She'd have had to climb over it."

The police woman frowned. "Red flowers?"

Lily Rose nodded. "Them fake flowers she keeps in that window box up there." She nodded toward Jessie's house and reached inside the damp crevice of her bosom for a small red box. Everything came to a stop as Lily Rose put a pinch of its contents behind her bottom lip. The smell of the snuff made Eliza's nose twitch.

"That's when I knowed something was wrong—bad wrong," the maid said, twisting her mouth around. "When I seen that bathroom door ajar, I got as cold as a frog's behind . . . and sure 'nuf, there she was, sprawled out in that water deader'n a door nail!" Lily Rose took time to spit a brown stream. "You coulda knocked my eyes off with a stick. Don't reckon I'll ever quit shakin' . . . can't even remember how I got back downstairs and called for help, but I knowed I couldn't stay in there."

At Dorcas's suggestion they moved to the shade of her porch, and no one declined, Eliza noticed, when her neighbor brought out a large pitcher of ice water. Lily Rose Jenkins sat fanning herself with the morning paper while she answered questions. "Did you touch anything?" the officer asked. "How did you know she was dead?"

"Reckon I know dead when I see it!" Lily Rose said. The newspaper fan stopped in mid-arc. "And I don't never want to see it again!" The porch chair creaked as she shifted her bulk. "I didn't have to *touch* her—her face was under the water . . . and that hair! Her hair was all floating around her like a mess of red mud!"

"Looks like she slipped and hit her head while getting out of the tub," Kemper Mungo told Eliza when he stopped by a little later. "Her nightgown was on the floor by the tub like she'd just stepped out of it, and a robe was hanging on the back of the door. Probably happened yesterday morning, but we don't know yet for sure."

"You mean she's just been lying there all this time?" Eliza remembered that several people had tried to telephone Jessie the day before. She had called a couple of times herself. Jessie Gilreath must have died about the same time Melody disappeared.

"Where did she hit her head?" she asked.

"I believe it was on the right side near the back. There was a puddle of water on the floor, and what was left of a bar of soap in the water. We think it must've happened when she tried to get out of the tub." Kemper avoided her eyes. "Apparently the blow knocked her out, and she drowned."

"But you don't really believe that, do you?" Eliza said.

"A little too much of a coincidence, you mean? But why would anybody want to kill Mrs. Gilreath?"

"I can see you didn't know her," Sydney said. "Jessie Gilreath wouldn't give you air if you were in a jug . . . but most of us were used to her. I guess everybody's wanted to knock Jessie into next week at one time or another, but I don't know of anyone who would go so far as to kill her."

"It had to be somebody she trusted," Kemper pointed out. "Or else they knew where she kept that key. There was no sign of forced entry—nothing out of place. If she was anything like you say she was, seems like she'd have put up a fight."

The three of them sat in the kitchen where Eliza peeled vegetables for a salad for lunch while Mattie napped upstairs. From the window over the sink Eliza could see her father weeding her mother's rose bed; his face was red from the heat. She had asked him to come inside twice, but he only shook his head. "I need to do something with my hands," he said. Eliza understood and felt the same. The waiting was like a contradiction in terms: a heavy emptiness, and she felt as if she had to be busy every minute until they heard from Melody.

The blood on the baby's blanket was O negative, the same as Melody's, Kemper Mungo had told them, but they didn't have results of the handwriting analysis yet. Today's searchers had found nothing in or around the river to indicate Melody had drowned—which must mean she was still alive. Eliza thought of Melody as being alive, and if she was, she would come back. If Melody Lamb were being held hostage, she would fight and claw —even crawl her way to freedom if she had to, to get back home to Mattie.

Eliza Figg knew love when she saw it, and for all Melody's strange ways, she was a good mother, and would never willingly leave her child. Eliza had told Kemper Mungo that. She now told him again.

"Think about it," Eliza said, whacking the end off a carrot. "Just before she took that last bath, Jessie Gilreath was standing at the window rearranging her little plastic garden. Somebody interrupted her . . . and she died. Why?"

"Because she saw something," Sydney and Kemper said together.

Jessie's upstairs window looked out on Habersham Street. From where she stood, she probably could see three houses within her range on the other side of the road: the Figgs', Dorcas Youngblood's, and the Thornbroughs'. "Didn't Randy Fossett say he heard The Boss barking about the time Melody passed his house?" Eliza said.

Kemper nodded. "It's possible, I guess, that Mrs. Gilreath saw something going on at the Thornbroughs', something that would excite the dog."

Syd drummed her fingers on the table. "Like a petal falling from a flower, the wind blowing through the grass . . . That stupid dog barks at everything and nothing!"

"Barked," Eliza reminded her. "He won't be barking anymore."

"That's *right*—the garbage truck got him!" Sydney crunched on a piece of carrot.

Kemper leaned forward and frowned. "What's that?"

"He ran in front of the truck," Eliza said. "About the same time Melody disappeared."

"And Jessie decided to rearrange her flowers . . ." Sydney looked from one to the other. "Jessie saw The Boss get out of his pen."

"Or she saw somebody *let* him out," Eliza said. "I remember seeing a garbage truck yesterday while I was looking for them. It was over on one of those little cul-de-sacs. I even *asked* the man if he'd seen them."

"Did you see the dog, hear him?" Kemper asked.

"No, and I'm sure I would have noticed him." Eliza gave the salad a toss. "I wonder where it happened."

Kemper reached for the kitchen phone. "I wonder *when*. Are the Thornbroughs back from vacation?"

"Don't think so, haven't seen them," Eliza said.

"Then I'll check with the Department of Sanitation. Maybe somebody will remember hitting the dog."

"Wait a minute," Syd said. "Why would anybody deliberately let The Boss out? It doesn't make sense."

"Yes, it does!" Now Eliza realized what had eluded her before. "If they knew Melody was terrified of that dog . . . and that it would chase her." She turned to Kemper. "Remember when I told you Melody would never get into a car with strangers?"

He made an effort to smile. "As if it were yesterday."

"Well, I think there was an exception." Eliza looked at Sydney and saw that she understood. "Melody would jump in the car with Jack the Ripper himself to get away from that dog."

"Which means somebody knew her schedule," Syd said. "Somebody must have been waiting for her out there. They *planned* to kidnap Melody."

Eliza watched her father fasten the toolshed door, heard him turn on the outside hydrant to wash his hands. A normal summer routine—she had seen him do it many times, but nothing was normal now. Someone had taken Melody, probably within a few blocks of home, and she didn't have the vaguest notion where she was.

Eliza looked across the table at Sydney. "She tried to tell us," she said. "I think she knew all along something was going to happen."

Kemper Mungo still stood with one hand on the phone. "But why? Why would anybody want to take Melody?"

Upstairs in her crib Melody's baby cried for attention. Maybe she would be next.

CHAPTER FOURTEEN

"Sit down, Eliza. You've looked in on that baby at least four times. Mattie's fine," Dorcas said. "If whoever did this wanted the baby, they'd have taken her along with Melody."

They sat on the Figgs' front porch with the door open, in case Mattie waked or made the slightest noise. Ben Figg leaned back in the rocking chair with his feet on the porch railing. Eliza and Dorcas shared the swing. Dark oak leaves blocked the glare of the street light, and partially hid the quiet house across the road. If she leaned a little to the right, Eliza could see the outline of the upstairs window where Jessie Gilreath had taken what was probably her last look at Habersham Street.

"Penny Shillinglaw knows something," Eliza said. "She's squirming like a worm in hot ashes."

"That girl always walks like she fixing to wet her pants," Dorcas said. "What makes you think she knows something?"

Eliza told them about Penny's peculiar behavior that

morning. "And she's the only one who could even get near The Boss—except for the Thornbroughs. Think about it."

Ben Figg turned to look at her. "You think the little Shillinglaw girl *let the dog out?* For God's sake, Eliza! Why would she do that?"

"Who knows? For money, maybe. Syd says she's saving for a car."

"We don't even know for sure if Jessie Gilreath was murdered, much less why," he said.

"Kemper Mungo thinks she was," Eliza told him.

"Well, he didn't say anything about it to me; I think you're jumping to conclusions." Her father's voice grew gentle. "Eliza, you're going to have to accept the possibility that Melody might have taken her own life."

"If Melody Lamb is dead, it wasn't her own doing. I know it." Eliza took a deep breath and tried to imagine where Melody might be: tied to a chair in a motel room somewhere; locked inside a musty closet. "And wherever she is, she'll try to get word to us somehow—if she's alive."

"She did leave the baby's shoes out there on the church walk to lead us to Mattie," Dorcas remembered.

"And what about the blood on the blanket?" Eliza watched her father's face. "Don't you think she was trying to tell us something?"

"What do you mean?"

"That something was wrong—that somebody was forcing her to do this. I think it was a signal for help."

Ben stared silently ahead. "I don't know . . . maybe. I just don't want you to get your hopes up." His feet hit the floor with a thud. "I'm going inside for a minute. Anybody want a glass of water or anything?"

Eliza knew her father was going in the house to call Olivia. Why didn't he just say so? It was the first lull they had had all day after the gruesome discovery across the street, and all the people coming and going at their own house. Eliza had enough cake in the freezer for a wedding reception, and she didn't know how they could possibly eat all those congealed salads.

Dorcas spoke softly. "You really think she'll come back?"

"If she can—I'm sure she will. But, Dorcas, why was she taken? We have to find out."

Dorcas covered Eliza's hand with her own. "I'd let the police do that, Honey. London wasn't built in a day, you know. That young man seems to know what he's doing."

But he's not doing it fast enough, Eliza thought. And she wasn't sure Kemper Mungo went along with her theory about Jessie's death.

The squeaking of the swing, usually a comforting noise, grated on her nerves, and Eliza walked to the edge of the porch. Honeysuckle had become entangled in her mother's forsythia, and the sweet smell of it gentled the night. Now and then lightning bugs winked on the lawn. She propped against the porch column and closed her eyes. If everything had gone as planned, she would be canoeing in Canada this very minute. The trip had been scheduled for almost two years, but Eliza couldn't afford to leave her job. She mopped away a trickle of sweat. It was probably cool up in Canada. Would Melody still be here if she had gone? The swing squeaked again, but Eliza was glad Dorcas was sitting there. She knew she probably relied on her neighbor too much since her mother died, but her presence lent a normalcy to the crazy things going on around them.

"Tell me what you think about this," Eliza said. "I believe Melody started out on her morning walk as usual, but this time somebody was waiting for her. They waited until she got out of sight of the house before they let the dog out . . ."

"You say *they*? You think there was more than one?"

"Had to be," Eliza said. "Somebody had to drive while the other person kept Melody from getting away. Penny says she wasn't here that day, but I think she knows something about it." She slapped at a mosquito. "Anyway, one of them must've noticed Jessie up there watching, and they knew they'd have to get rid of her *right then* before she told somebody what she'd seen."

"Eliza Figg, you know as well as I do Jessie would never open her door to a stranger."

"Maybe it wasn't a stranger, or maybe they told her some wild tale and she believed it . . . or they could have known where she kept that key."

The swing grew still. "And they just walked right in and drowned her?" Dorcas didn't sound convinced.

"No, they probably hit her first—knocked her out, then put her in the tub so it would look like an accident."

"By golly, either you're beginning to make sense, or I'm losing what little dab of gray matter I've got left. But what did they do with the dog all this time?"

"Don't know. I haven't figured that out yet, but they must have had a leash or something. Maybe they gave it a bone—lured it into the car somehow," Eliza said.

"And then turned it loose so they could 'rescue' Melody." Dorcas Youngblood's voice sounded very far away.

"It must have happened sometime after she turned onto Henry Grady Street. Kemper told me the garbage truck didn't hit The Boss until it was way up there on Lanier Lane, and that's a dead end; they turn around up there. Said the dog ran right out in front of them . . . wasn't any way they could keep from hitting it."

"How did they know whose dog it was?" Dorcas asked.

"Traced it by it's tags. They couldn't leave it lying there, but the vet knew it was the Thornbroughs' dog." Eliza tugged at a honeysuckle vine that encircled the porch railing. "That must've happened just before I saw the sanitation truck that morning. The whole time I was talking to that man, The Boss was lying there dead in the truck.

"Of course it wouldn't have done any good to know it. By then, Mattie was already parked in front of the Episcopal chapel, and Melody was on her way to . . . wherever they meant to take her."

Dorcas sighed as she stood, leaving the porch swing swaying behind her. "Well, it's been a long day, I'd better get on home, and you ought to go inside too, Eliza, before these blasted mosquitoes eat you alive." Still, she hesitated at the steps. "Now, look, I don't want you to take this wrong, but have you ever stopped to think maybe Melody might have planned all this herself? You'll have to admit she was different, didn't act like anybody I ever knew." Dorcas shook her head. "I just couldn't get close to Melody."

"I know; nobody could. And yes, I have thought of it, but I just can't see her leaving that baby the way she did. I think Melody left Mattie there because she didn't have a choice, and because it was the safest place available at the time."

Eliza followed her neighbor down the front steps and stood with her on the uneven walk of long-broken octagonal stones. "But it was the blood," she said, "that makes me feel sure Melody's in trouble. I think she scratched herself or something—put it there on purpose—to let us know she needed help."

Baxter Phillips called as Eliza was getting ready for bed. "Any news yet?" he asked.

"You probably know as much as I do." Eliza knew he had been one of the volunteers to search the area where Melody's clothes were found. "We haven't heard a thing, but I still don't think Melody's in that river . . . do you?"

He took his time in answering. "Hard to say, Eliza. I hope not, but if she is, we ought to know something before too long."

Hard to say. Wasn't that what everybody said when they didn't want to answer? Couldn't they guess by now that Melody hadn't thrown herself in the rushing brown waters of the Etowah? Why weren't they looking for the reason she was gone?

"I can't stand around here waiting any longer," Eliza told him. "I've got to find the real Melody. The Melody who existed before she came back to Minerva. And why she was so afraid."

"How do you mean to do that?" She could tell by his voice he wasn't taking her seriously.

"A lot of Melody's things are in storage in Atlanta, things she didn't have room for in that little apartment. Most of it belongs to her mother, the one who's in the nursing home. I'm hoping there's something there . . . anything! There has to be."

"And then what?" he said.

"What do you mean?" Eliza yawned. She hadn't thought she would ever be sleepy again.

"If Melody doesn't come back . . . what about the baby?"

"I'll take care of her, of course. I promised. Who else would raise her? Mattie doesn't have any relatives."

"Thought you said Melody's husband had family in Tennessee? What about Sonny's mother? His brothers and sisters? Don't they have a say in this?"

"Look, Melody's had two letters and a crocheted baby blanket from Sonny's mother since January. That's all. Besides, Mattie doesn't even know them!" Eliza hung up the telephone feeling as if she'd just eaten a huge bowl of chili from hell. Her stomach burned clear up to her chest. Baxter Phillips didn't have to worry about what would become of Mattie. It wasn't his problem. She knew it never would be.

"By God, Eliza, you're not going!" Ben Figg said. "You are not gallivanting off to Atlanta by yourself poking about where you don't belong. Especially after what's happened to Melody."

Eliza looked at the floor so he wouldn't see her grin. When her father started saying "By God," she knew he had moved out of the realm of reasoning. She also knew she would go in spite of him. Ben Figg knew it too.

"I won't be going alone. Syd's coming with me."

"Eddie McClanahan's gonna leave her high and dry if she doesn't quit running off and leaving him to take care of all those children. Oughta stay home where she belongs . . . and so should you."

"Oink!" Eliza said. "Oink! Oink!" It was her way of reminding him he was acting like a chauvinist pig. "What would your Olivia say if she could hear how you talk? I thought they were Eddie's kids too."

Actually it was Eddie's soft-hearted mother who would be stuck with the children for most of the day, but she wasn't going to tell him that now.

Her father almost smiled. "You know very well what I mean. Hell, I'll go with you myself! Olivia can stay here with Mattie."

"That's two cuss words already, and on a Sunday too," Eliza reminded him. "I sure hope Mama isn't listening." Eliza took her father's hands. "I'd rather you stay here, really. What if we heard from Melody? And it'll give you and Olivia a chance to be alone for a few hours while you babysit." She kissed his cheek and saw by his eyes he was pleased. "We won't be late, I promise, and Dorcas will be right next door if you need her."

"How do you know where we're going?" Syd asked a few minutes later when Eliza came by for her. Eliza looked at her in amazement as she slid into the seat beside her. She had never seen another person who could squirm into sandals, button a shirt, and brush her hair at the same time.

"The key and the name of the place were in an envelope in Melody's desk. She showed it to me one time. I had to look through her receipts for the address."

Syd glanced at her sideways. "Find anything else?"

"Nothing significant, at least nothing that dates back more than a few months. I just hope we'll know what's important when we find it."

"I wish you'd tell me what we're looking for," Syd said

later as they picked their way through the small shed piled with furniture and cartons. "If I'd known it was going to be this hot in here, I'd have brought along potatoes for supper. I'm about half-baked already."

Eliza looked at her across a leaning stack of kitchen chairs. "I always *knew* that!" She untied the string from a box labeled *shoes* and groaned.

Sydney frowned. "What is it? What'd you find?"

"Shoes. Just shoes. Must've belonged to Mrs. Sutherland." Eliza put the box back where she'd found it. "Wish we could find some annuals, old letters, anything like that."

"Look, here's something!" Syd shook out a wrinkled wad of blue and orange fabric.

"What is it—other than being ugly? A bathing suit?"

"No, silly, it's a cheerleading uniform. Can't you see the skirt? And it has letters on the front: GJHS." Sydney held the tiny dress to her chest. "Can you imagine Melody as a cheerleader?"

"Not the Melody we knew," Eliza said. "Must've been junior high. See if you can reach that box there behind you. Maybe we can find some pictures."

"You're still not sure, are you?" Syd asked as she smoothed the uniform in its packing box.

"Sure about what?"

"Melody. That she's who she says she is."

"Just when she had me convinced, she'd do or say something that made me doubt her." Eliza told Syd what Melody had said about playing with the gray kitten. "You *know* we never had a gray kitten."

"No, but the Youngbloods did—remember? Dorcas just called it Scat. Melody used to dress it in doll clothes."

Eliza wiped moisture from her face with the tail of her shirt. "Lord, I'd forgotten that. Still, I don't guess there's any way to be sure . . . but look at this stuff, Sydney: just your ordinary run-of-the-mill furniture. This is what Dorcas would call *Early Attic*. The Sutherlands didn't have any money. If our Melody was pretending, it wasn't because of this!"

"If *our* Melody was pretending," Sydney said, "what happened to the real Melody?"

But Eliza had inched her way to a wooden box almost hidden beneath a huge electric fan. When she raised the lid and looked inside, she must have let out a yell, because Syd vaulted over a tower of books to reach her. "What is it?" Syd asked. "What have you found?"

"I don't think we need to worry about the real Melody anymore," Eliza said. And she lifted out the hairless naked doll that was Victoria Antoinette.

Chapter Fifteen

"Yeah?" Sydney just stood there with her hands on her hips. "Well?"

"Well, what? Don't you recognize her?"

"What? You mean the doll?" Syd ran a gentle finger over the doll's delicate features. "Good Lord! It is, isn't it? Poor Victoria Antoinette—she looks like she's been scalped."

"No wonder Melody didn't remember her the way she was." Eliza wrapped her old doll in a frayed blanket scrap.

"So you're convinced she's really Melody?"

"I don't know what else to think. Obviously all these things belonged to the family that adopted Melody, and that *is* the doll I gave her. Now it's beginning to add up." Eliza stuck the doll under her arm and shoved the box aside. "Why wouldn't she be?"

Sydney brushed grimy hands on her shorts. "Can we talk about this on the way home? It must be one hundred ten degrees in here, and it would take forever to go through all this stuff."

"Right. Just let me get the box on top of that dresser there. It's full of papers—could be photographs, and there's another in that stack by the door. Guess I can look at some of these things at home."

Eliza waited until the air conditioner in her car was going full blast before she mentioned the subject again. "Now, tell me what you meant back there? How could Mattie's mother be anyone else but Melody Lamb?"

"Easy." Syd leaned forward and let the cool air blow through her damp hair. "Anybody who knew Melody well or had access to her things could have the key to that storage unit. Melody's dad is dead and Mrs. Sutherland wouldn't know the difference right now. Even if she did, she's not able to tell anybody."

"Would you mind if we stopped by there for a minute, or are you in a big hurry?" Eliza asked.

"You mean the nursing home?" Syd frowned. "We don't look much like Sunday company."

"I doubt if Mrs. Sutherland will notice, and it's on the way. Besides, somebody should check on her."

Syd leaned back and sighed. "What are you looking for, Eliza? Think you'll find Melody hiding under the bed?"

Melody Lamb wasn't underneath her mother's bed at the Apple Blossom Convalescent Center, but a recent photograph of the Melody Eliza knew sat on a dresser in Susan Sutherland's room. The older woman seemed restless and was incapable of speech, so Eliza and Syd stayed only long enough to feed her an afternoon treat of frozen yogurt and vanilla wafers and to ask if she needed anything from the store.

"No, Melody took care of that when she was here last week," the nurse told them. "Don't suppose you've heard any more?"

She shook her head tearfully when Eliza said they were waiting to hear about the handwriting.

"I was off Friday, the day she disappeared," the woman said. "And when I saw that in the paper the next day—why, I just went as weak as dishwater! I reckon I saw that girl just about every week, and you can't tell me she'd deliberately go off and leave her baby like that!"

Eliza nodded sympathetically. She didn't believe it either, she said.

But the note found in Mattie's stroller was written by Melody Lamb, Kemper Mungo told her when he called the next day. The expert who analyzed it wasn't a hundred percent sure, he said, but there were definite indications the "suicide" note and the samples Eliza sent were written by the same person.

The policeman paused, and Eliza sensed he wanted to tell her more.

"What is it, Kemper? Tell me. What else did they say?"

"Probably nothing you didn't guess already," he said. "But from the boldness of the letters, the fact that she was bearing down when she wrote them, he thinks Melody was writing under stress."

"You're right, that doesn't tell us a lot, does it? So where do we go from here?" Eliza knew they had found nothing when they dragged the river on Saturday, and there were no reports of a suspicious black car anywhere in the area.

"This isn't television, you know. You can't always solve a major crime in an hour. Believe me, we're putting this first. It just takes time."

"Melody doesn't have time! She may be . . ." Shut up, Eliza! You've riled him already, and you want this man on your side. "Look, I'm sorry, Kemper, it's just that I have a very strong feeling Melody's still alive, but she might not be for long. What about Jessie Gilreath? When will you have the results of her autopsy?"

"They didn't request an autopsy on Mrs. Gilreath, Eliza." His voice was calm, but he wasn't. She could tell.

"Why on earth not?"

"Because the coroner considers it an accident. There was no sign of foul play."

"But the dog—did you tell them about the dog? And it

happened the *same time* Melody disappeared. You can't tell me that's coincidence, Kemper Mungo." Damn! She'd done it again. Oh, to hell with it!

He sighed. Well, it was more like a moan. "We're talking to everybody in the neighborhood, Eliza. Anyone who might have noticed something, no matter how trivial it might seem."

"Have you talked with Penny Shillinglaw?" Eliza asked.

He didn't know who she was, so she had to explain. "She's the only person who wasn't afraid of The Boss, and she acted . . . well, definitely spooky when I asked her about that morning. I think she knows something."

"What do you mean?"

"About how the dog got out, and Melody disappeared. She's *antsy*—well, nervous. Almost guilty. There's something she's not telling. I think you should talk with her."

"Tell me about her," Kemper said. And she did.

She heard him tapping, tapping on the desk with his fingernails. "Will you go with me?" he said.

"Me? Where?"

"To see this girl. What's her name . . . Penny something or other?"

"Why me?"

"You know her, don't you? What would you think if you were seventeen . . . eighteen . . . how old is she, anyway? And this strange policeman suddenly started asking questions of you?"

"I see what you mean," Eliza said. "When?"

"Pick you up in thirty minutes." She was listening to a dial tone.

"Don't worry, they're expecting us," Kemper said as they got out of the car in front of the Shillinglaws' neat stucco home.

Eliza wasn't worried, but she could see that Kemper was a little uneasy about questioning a young girl while her mother stood guard with her arms folded. Penny stationed herself on the other side of the room, as far away from them as she could get, and bit her lip as if she wanted to trap the words inside. She looked almost naked, Eliza thought, without either a telephone or a headset. When Mrs. Shillinglaw finally asked them to sit down, Penny silently took her place on the arm of her mother's chair.

Kemper began with a smile, but Eliza could tell it didn't do a bit of good. "I hope you don't mind our dropping by," he said. "But frankly, we could use your help."

"Oh? And how is that?" Penny's mother glanced at her daughter with a look that said, *What have you been up to now?*

"I understand you sometimes feed the Thornbroughs' dog when they're away," he said to Penny. "I wondered if you might have been in the neighborhood last Friday when Melody Lamb disappeared."

"I told Eliza I was at the dentist's that morning!" Penny twisted the class ring on her finger. It was her own ring, Eliza noticed. Not a boy's.

"At seven o'clock in the morning?" Kemper made the question sound light, as though the whole thing were a joke, but Eliza knew he was dead serious.

"Penny sees Dr. Freeman in Atlanta," the girl's mother said. "She had an eight-thirty appointment; I drove her there myself." She didn't add, *So there!* She didn't have to.

Kemper nodded. "I see. Would you know of anyone else who might be friendly with the dog—other than yourself? Is it possible the Thornbroughs would have asked someone else to take care of him since you weren't going to be in town that day?" He directed his question to Penny, but her mother answered instead.

"Wait a minute! Isn't that the day The Boss was hit by that truck? Surely you aren't blaming that on Penny?"

"No, of course not. But there's a possibility that whoever came to feed The Boss might have accidently left the gate open. We're hoping they might have noticed something else as well." Kemper seemed so patient, Eliza thought. How could he be this calm? The woman was a pit viper ready to strike.

"The Boss never ate in the morning. I told you that," Penny said, frowning at Eliza. "When I came over to feed him that afternoon, he was gone. I found out later he'd been hit by that truck."

"So you don't know of anyone who might have stopped—just to pet him or something?" Kemper asked. "A neighbor maybe?"

Penny Shillinglaw shrugged. "The neighbors hated The Boss. He wouldn't let anybody in there but the Thornbroughs and me . . . unless . . ."

"Unless what?" Eliza said.

"Unless somebody gave him a bone or something. He specially liked ham bones."

"Did anybody else know that?" Kemper said.

Penny stood suddenly. "How should I know? Ask the Thornbroughs. He was their dog."

"See what I mean?" Eliza said as they drove back to the Figgs'. "That girl was so jittery I thought she was going to cry."

"She did cry. At least I think she did. Didn't you see her run out of the room? Maybe it was because she was upset over the dog."

"I don't think so," Eliza said. "Why would she be so nervous? Practically hostile."

"Well, at least she gave us something to go on," he said.

"I didn't notice. What?"

"The ham bone. If somebody did give that dog a ham bone, there's a slight chance it might still be around," Kemper said. "It's worth a look, anyway."

Eliza shook her head. "You're actually going to scout the neighborhood for a *ham bone?*"

"Strictly in a supervisory capacity, you understand. I've got two nephews who will do almost anything for a buck."

"Well, golly—sorry I won't be able to help you there," Eliza said, "but I don't see my dad's car in the driveway. Guess I'd better go see where he's gone."

Eliza found Benjamin Figg giving Mattie a bath in the kitchen sink. He looked almost domestic with one of Martha Figg's aprons tied around his newly trim waist, but he seemed preoccupied about something. "I'd hug you, but my hands are wet," he said with a glancing kiss at Eliza's cheek. "Besides, I can't let go this Tootie Squat."

Eliza smiled. Her dad had labeled Mattie a "Tootie Squat" baby from the very beginning, but only he knew what the nickname meant. "Some babies are Tootie Squats and some aren't," he said. "You were one yourself, Eliza. If I have to explain, you wouldn't understand."

Eliza handed Ben a towel and watched him swathe the dripping infant. "You don't *rub* a baby dry like that, Daddy, you *pat*. You'll take her skin off." She sat at the table across from him and kicked off her sandals. "Didn't see your car. Where's Olivia?" Why wouldn't he look at her?

"Had to get back to Atlanta. I'll be along in a day or two . . . need to see C. C. Reece to take care of a few details." Ben Figg looked at his daughter over the baby's fuzzy head. "Besides, it gives me a chance to play with Mattie."

"You don't have to babysit me, Daddy. Really. I'm a big girl now."

"That doesn't keep me from worrying. What about today? Learn anything new?"

"Not much. It doesn't look good, but I know she didn't kill herself. Somebody kidnapped Melody, just don't ask me why!"

"Either that, or she planned this herself," Ben Figg said.

Eliza was pouring orange juice into a bottle for Mattie, and it dribbled onto the floor. "What on earth makes you think that?"

"Because . . ." Ben Figg frowned, and then he did

something that was most unusual for him. He fidgeted—
or came as close to it as Eliza had ever seen him.

"Because what? What is the matter with you, Daddy?"

"Because Olivia thinks she saw her! This afternoon in
Dogwood Park—on the other side of Atlanta; there's a
walking trail there, and you know how Livvy is about her
exercise! Anyway, she phoned me as soon as she got
home—said she could've sworn she saw Melody Lamb
on the path in front of her. Even called to her, Livvy said,
but Melody didn't answer."

CHAPTER SIXTEEN

"The woman exaggerates," Dorcas Youngblood said. "You know how Olivia is."

"But what if it's true?" Eliza stood at the window watching the late June twilight darken into night.

"If it's true, if Melody really did plan this, do you think she'd take a chance on being seen?"

"Maybe she hit her head or something. Maybe she doesn't remember."

"And maybe she's been taken by space aliens to another galaxy," Dorcas said with a beginning of a smile.

"Okay, let's say she doesn't have amnesia," Eliza said. "Dogwood Park must be over a hundred miles from here. Late on a Monday afternoon, what are the chances somebody from Minerva would decide to hike there? Melody . . . if it was Melody, probably thought she was safe."

"Well, if it was Melody, we should hear from her soon. Meanwhile, I think you'd better get on with your life, honey. We're all on edge living day to day like this."

"If somebody would tell me how *not* to, I'd promise to

give it a try," Eliza said. "But you do have a point. Syd and I talked about it this afternoon."

"And what did you and Sydney decide?" Ben Figg came in from watering what was left of the flowers and went directly to the refrigerator.

"That you need to get back to work, and so do I," Eliza told him. "Like Dorcas just said, we should get on with our lives."

Her father backed out of the refrigerator with both hands loaded for salad. "I don't trust you, Eliza. I love you, but I don't trust you. As soon as my back is turned, you'll be out God knows where playing Indiana Jones!"

Eliza laughed. "Come on, I'm not really into whips. For heaven's sake, Daddy, you can't stay here forever and have poor old Olivia running back and forth all the time. Dorcas is right next door, and I'll be at Bellawood most of the day. I'll be fine." And frankly, she'd just as soon have Olivia stay put in Atlanta where she belonged, Eliza thought.

Her father reached for the familiar earthenware bowl and held it in both hands as if it gave him comfort. "I know it's hard for you having us here—Livvy too. I hope in time you'll feel more relaxed together."

Eliza doubted if she'd live that long, but the desperate look on his face made her ache. "I promised I'd try, and I will. I hope Olivia knows she's welcome." *Like a slug in a garden salad!*

Eliza turned away. Could he tell what she was thinking? She really was going to have to start trying a little harder to make peace with Olivia.

The two boxes she had brought from storage the day before were stacked in the corner where she'd left them. Now would be a good time to go through them; it would give them something to do, and she could use the help. After Dorcas left, Eliza pulled one into the middle of the floor. "I'm doing a little detective work, wanna give me a hand?"

"Fine, what are we looking for?" Ben tossed his book aside.

"Pictures. Pictures of Melody. I want to see the in-between stage, the emergence of the Melody we know now. There was a photograph in her mother's room at the nursing home," Eliza said, "but it's recent. Melody could've put it there any time. Susan Sutherland wouldn't know the difference."

He shook his head. "You're still not convinced the woman who came here is the same one we knew as a child?"

"I just want to be sure. That box looks like it has yearbooks in it. Why don't you look through those? I'll dig into this other one."

When the phone rang a few minutes later he had started on the second in the stack. The first one listed Melody's name, he said, but she must not have had her picture taken that year.

"Figures." Eliza stepped over his long legs to get to the phone.

"Guess what my clever nephews found?" Kemper Mungo said.

"Don't tell me . . . a ham bone!"

"Well, actually they found three," he said. "But one was a lot fresher than the rest, even had a little meat on it still."

"Where'd they find it?"

"In the ditch in front of the Thornbroughs' place, right out next to the street. It had rolled into some of that plant that spreads. What's the name of that stuff?"

"Juniper," Eliza said. "So, they bribed him with a big, fat, juicy ham bone, then made him drop it before they got him into the car. Bet The Boss didn't like that much." Eliza lowered her voice. "Jessie must've seen them; wouldn't surprise me if she yelled at them from the window."

"Hmm . . . well . . . just thought I'd let you know,"

he said. "And about Jessie—you'll be glad to know they've decided on an autopsy after all."

Eliza wondered who, or what, made them change their minds. She hung up the phone concocting a fable for her father. Ben Figg would be sure to ask who had called, and why. He liked to make fun of Jessie Gilreath, but he was almost as nosy as she had been. It wouldn't do for him to know Eliza was one step closer to being right about the way their neighbor had died.

But Ben didn't look up; in fact, he didn't seem to be curious at all. Eliza watched him study the book on his lap and run a finger down the page. "I think I've found what we're looking for," he said, holding the annual to the light. "Come over here and see."

"That's her all right," Eliza said. "Sure looks like Melody to me."

"And there's another over here." Ben flipped back a few pages. "President of the Young Gourmets—wouldn't you know it?"

Eliza smiled. "How old do you suppose she was then?"

"I don't know . . . sixteen, seventeen. This was her junior year." Benjamin Figg looked up at her, his finger marking the page. "Well, does this answer your question?"

Eliza kissed his cheek and nodded. "I reckon it does. What do you say we celebrate with a dish of ice cream?"

Her father's eyes brightened, then he shook his head. "I really shouldn't . . . oh, what the hell! You won't tell Livvy, will you?"

Eliza smiled as she hugged him. "This time it will be our secret."

"Whatever Olivia's doing with your diet, it seems to be paying off," Eliza told her father the next morning as she left for work. "I don't mean to be a bad influence, so promise you'll stay with it, okay?" As much as Eliza hated to admit it, her father looked younger than he had in years, and she knew it was because of Olivia.

Beatrice Tutwiler would be traveling in New England for several weeks, so Dorcas had agreed to look after Mattie. Olivia had reported seeing Melody to Minerva's Police Chief Milton Asbury, but they still hadn't heard anything from Melody, or from the police, and Eliza felt strange driving to Bellawood as if nothing had changed.

She walked through the quiet old house feeling like a ghost of herself. It was impossible to grasp the changes in her life in less than a week. Melody was gone. Really gone, and if she never came back, the baby would be hers to raise.

Eliza loved Mattie, wanted her, but the reality of her situation scared her to death. Other people took babies everywhere. She had seen them in their little papooselike carriers on cyclists and hikers, even in remote camping areas. Well, she could do that too. But what if Sonny's relatives claimed guardianship? She had talked with his mother over the phone after Melody turned up missing, and the woman had seemed concerned, even distraught over Melody's disappearance. She had asked about the baby, but so far had not brought up the subject of Mattie's future.

Eliza didn't want to think about a future without Mattie.

She couldn't sit still. Docents wandered in with sympathetic faces. Genevieve Ellison brought warm poppy-seed bread and a Thermos of tea and left them on Eliza's desk with a light touch of her hand. Genevieve was tall and bony and walked with her head jutting forward as if she had a mission in life and was eager to get on with it. Now and then she poked her long, kind face in the doorway, then loped off somewhere else as if she'd forgotten something. Eliza thanked her silently; it was all she could manage for the time being.

Eliza measured the day in tasks; tasks and rewards.

Thirty minutes of letter writing earned a cup of tea and a stretch; an hour of mailing brochures warranted a prowl through the house. She began writing a lecture for next week's Friends of the Library social, but couldn't concentrate on it. By midafternoon Genevieve and the remaining docent had removed themselves to the shady end of the front porch. From an open window of the bedroom upstairs, Eliza, wandering through, heard the low hum of their voices and the steady roll of rocking chairs. They reminded her of people at a funeral, respectful and subdued.

The limp curtain moved in a feeble breeze, and Eliza stood by the window to take advantage of it.

". . . a strange one, all right," the younger docent said. "From what I've heard, wouldn't surprise me if she did turn up in that river. You know what rivers are like . . . could be snagged on something."

"Let's hope not," Genevieve said quietly.

Bless you, Eliza thought, looking down at them. She wanted to scream at the other woman: *Melody did not kill herself!* Why did everyone want to accept the easiest solution? Eliza knew it wasn't true. And Kemper Mungo knew it too.

The pastel likeness of Pentecost's young wife, Lucy, hung over the carved four-poster. Except for a rose-painted pitcher, it was the only bright spot in the room. Looking at her, Eliza allowed her thoughts to wander back to another time—a time before Melody disappeared, before Jessie Gilreath looked out on something she shouldn't have seen.

Lucy had allowed her light brown curls to escape in tendrils about her face, and her dark eyes held a hint of something. Humor? Determination? Both, probably. Eliza wondered what it must have been like to share a home with the formidable Bella. And she had mothered all those children before anyone even thought about inventing a washing machine, or a dryer. Or penicillin.

Two of her babies lay in small graves behind the family chapel.

Mattie. Eliza started back to her office. She would just give Dorcas a call and see how things were going.

She got no farther than the doorway when the telephone started to ring, and for some reason it sounded unusually demanding. Eliza hurried to answer.

"Didn't know whether I ought to call you or not, but then I thought you'd want to know. *I'd* want to know . . ."

"Know what? Who is this?" Why did everybody in Minerva think you could identify them instantly by their voices?

"Why it's Brenda! Brenda Grayson, your old classmate; only I was Brenda Craig back then. Don't tell me you've forgotten me already, Eliza.

"Listen, I'm real sorry about what happened. I called your house and your neighbor—or somebody—told me you were here."

Eliza remembered Brenda Craig. She always wrote with purple ink and dotted her *i's* with little hearts. She was one of those who married as soon as she got out of high school and had three kids in about as many years.

"I started not to call," Brenda went on, "but the more I thought about it, the more I was sure it was her. It sure looked like that girl I saw you with in the A&P a couple of weeks ago. I was in there buying dog food, remember?"

Eliza remembered. "Where did you see her, Brenda?"

"Well, Tony—that's my middle one—had a ball game over at that park: Dogwood Park. You know, other side of Atlanta, and when we were getting ready to leave, I could've sworn I saw her in the parking lot."

"When was this?"

"Day before yesterday. They're in the play-offs, you know. Lasted all afternoon and the traffic was awful! I didn't think we'd ever get outa that place."

"Did you see what she was driving?" Eliza sat on the desk, scattering papers to the floor.

"Didn't look like she was driving anything," Brenda said. "When we finally left, I saw her walking out to the street. Looked like she'd just come over to jog or something."

"About what time, do you remember?"

"I don't know for sure. Late. After five."

About the same time Olivia had reported seeing Melody the day before. And in the same place. *Melody wasn't dead. She knew it.*

Eliza thanked Brenda for calling and told her that Kemper would probably be in touch. If they could just locate Melody, she would never sneer at her classmate's purple hearts again.

"Now, don't get your hopes up too much," Kemper said when she called him a few seconds later. "It could just be a look-alike, a coincidence."

"Don't give me that! Two different people have seen her in the same park a couple of days in a row. If you won't check it out, I will!" Eliza felt as though all her energy had drained into the telephone.

"Sounds like this woman's a jogger. Was Melody into that?" Come to think of it, he sounded kind of tired too.

"That's how she disappeared, remember? Melody walked every morning."

"But mostly for the baby's benefit, from what you've told me, and it's not the same as jogging. Look, I'll talk to Brenda, and to your uh-stepmother—compare notes. And we'll notify the police down there, circulate her photo, but it just doesn't make sense to me. What would Melody Lamb be doing in Dogwood Park?"

Eliza wondered too. And if the police didn't have any luck by the end of the week, she meant to find out for herself.

CHAPTER SEVENTEEN

"I'm not going back to that park with you again," Sydney announced. "It's been almost two weeks, Eliza. If Melody's there, don't you think the police would've seen her?"

"Not necessarily," Eliza said. "Brenda saw her on a Sunday, remember? Then Olivia said she was there the next day at about the same time."

"So?"

"It rained on both of those days this week. Remember how nasty it was? Nobody would get out in that, so of course nobody saw her!"

"But it didn't rain the rest of the time," Sydney said. "Where was she then?"

"I don't know. Maybe she only goes there on those two days. Besides, the police there wouldn't know her. Melody's not that distinctive."

"Exactly." Sydney folded her arms and looked appallingly superior. "That's what I've been trying to tell you. Those two saw somebody who *looked* like Melody. Look,

Eliza, I want Melody to be alive too, but I think you're snatching at thin air here. Besides, if she's able to jog around a park, she's able to call and let somebody know she's okay."

Eliza groaned. "You sound just like Kemper Mungo."

"Well, it does sort of blow our kidnapped theory," Syd admitted. "What did he say about Jessie? The way she died?"

"The medical examiner said she drowned. She could've slipped in the tub and hit her head; there's no way to prove she didn't, so I guess you could say the results were inconclusive."

Syd frowned. "In other words, they don't know."

"Right. And Kemper says it's the same way about the bone. Chief Asbury thinks he's exaggerating. 'What dog wouldn't like a ham bone?' he says."

Sydney thought about that as they sat on her back steps watching her four battle it out with water guns. "True, but what was the bone doing out by the road? Besides, if I were going to lure a dog, I'd probably go with a beef bone—the big kind you throw in the soup pot."

Eliza shrugged. "Still, he says it's just a theory, and the chief won't go on theories. He needs proof, Kemper says. Witnesses."

"Stop that, Mary Beth McClanahan! Not right in his *face!*" Sydney yelled. "Well," she added, turning to Eliza. "I'm afraid our only witness is dead . . . hey, where're you going?"

"Gotta run. Dorcas has a hot date: that wild bunch she runs with."

Syd lifted an eyebrow.

"The Crazy Quilters; they're headed for the mountains, and she hasn't packed. Told her I'd only be a few minutes."

"What do you hear from your dad?"

"Coming tomorrow. *Both of them.* Be here all day, I guess." Eliza sighed as she put her empty lemonade glass on the crayon-scarred porch table.

"You behave," Syd told her. "And be careful."

"Careful of what?" Eliza didn't dare meet her eyes.

"This is me: Sydney—remember? I know you're going to that park again tomorrow, Eliza Figg. Just watch your step, okay?"

There is no such thing as a harmless place, Olivia Figg had said when Eliza told her she was making another visit to Dogwood Park. Her stepmother guessed where she was going when she slipped away that afternoon, but Eliza swore her to secrecy and told her father she was going to a Braves game with friends. Now she twirled the dial on her radio as she walked the winding trails of the park. Better keep up with the score—just in case!

The thermometer in front of the Bank of Minerva had read ninety-two degrees, and Eliza wore the briefest shorts she could find and her hair pulled back in a pony tail beneath one of Ben Figg's old golfing hats. Strolling along with earphones clamped to her head, she looked like everybody else she met. And Dogwood Park seemed innocent enough swarming with picnicking families, children yelling and chasing one another. Now and then a cyclist passed her, or a jogger glistening with sweat. At six o'clock it was just as hot as it had been an hour before when Eliza started her vigil. How could anybody possibly stand to run in such heat?

Eliza took a swig from her water bottle and made a face. Even the water was hot. She sat on a large rock in comparative shade near the park's entrance and wiped her face. It would be almost impossible to pick out Melody from the other women here. Melody was so medium: medium weight, medium height, nondescript hair; only those huge eyes set her apart. But everyone seemed to be wearing sunglasses.

Eliza wished she had an apple, something to gnaw on so she wouldn't look so obvious sitting there doing nothing. Besides, she was hungry. She had only picked at the lunch she prepared for the new Mr. and Mrs. Benjamin

Figg. And it had been a good lunch too: marinated vegetables, mixed summer fruits with lemon and mint, cold
cuts and potato salad. Even the dainty Olivia had seconds.

It had been just the three of them and Mattie. Thank
God for Mattie! She had given them a focal point and
entertained them all with her attempts at crawling and
the funny faces she made. The baby could sit alone now
for a few seconds at a time before falling over like a sack
of flour. And Melody had missed it.

*Where are you, Melody Lamb? Life is going on without
you.* Eliza flicked a black ant from her leg and stood to
stretch. Melody wouldn't have missed a part of her
daughter's life intentionally. If it had been Melody the
two women had seen, it wasn't the Melody she knew.

Eliza stopped at the fountain to splash water on her
face. It was too warm to be refreshing. She thought of her
father back in Minerva eating cold watermelon on the
back porch. Ben and Olivia had bought one of those big
green striped ones on the way home from Atlanta, and
Eliza could almost taste the cool red sweetness of it.

And it was almost impossible to eat watermelon without getting it all over you. She smiled at the thought of
proper Olivia dripping with pink juice.

Sydney had lectured her the day before. "For heaven's
sake, Eliza! When are you going to forgive your dad for
marrying Olivia? It's been six months now."

"Hey, don't use your green witch voice with me,"
Eliza said.

"That's not what it's all about though, is it?" Syd per-
sisted. "You're still mad about Chris Wylie . . . aren't
you? My God, Eliza, that's been . . . what? Ten years at
least."

"Chris Wylie? Don't be silly! I haven't thought of him
in ages . . . well, not much, anyway. Wonder what happened to him?"

"Probably in jail somewhere—unless he ran that
souped-up car off the side of a mountain," Syd said.

"Come on now, can you really imagine being married to Chris? You'd end up supporting him, plus any little mini-Chrises that happened along."

"I don't believe he ever mentioned marriage," Eliza said. "But you'll have to admit he *was* good-looking."

"And then there was Spencer G. Fillmore, the wandering adventurer. Your dad must be continually thrilled. Where is old Spencer, by the way?"

"Get off my back, will you Syd? Not everybody's cut out for the domestic life. Besides, my parents never really flipped out over Spencer the way they did over Chris Wylie. Maybe they just gave up."

Sydney nodded. "So? Quit blaming your dad."

"Do I get a chance for rebuttal?"

"No. Everybody's mad at their parents about something. Mine never took me camping—and they wouldn't let me go on that class trip to the beach, remember?"

"You had mono, Syd."

"Minor detail. But I forgave them, didn't I? Get on with it, Eliza!"

Traitor. Eliza slogged along the dusty path, trying to stay in the shade. Syd had been just as shocked as she was when Ben Figg announced his marriage plans, and now she had gone over to the other side. Yet Eliza knew Syd was right. Somewhere in the back of her mind was the echo of a childish chant: *If I can't have Chris Wylie, you can't be happy with Olivia!* And she didn't even want Chris Wylie anymore. Spencer G. Fillmore was another matter. Maybe.

A group of teens played softball in a grassy area a few yards away. Eliza heard the crack of a bat, and the ball thumped against a tree beside the trail. She threw it back to the outfielder, wishing they would let her play too. She was hot, hungry and bored. And she wasn't sure her vigil was worth the effort. It was close to seven, and she hadn't seen anyone who faintly resembled Melody. Eliza headed for the rest room before she left for the long ride home.

It was in the stall next to hers that she saw the shorts: pink and purple plaid, like Melody wore. Eliza leaned over to look at thin ankles, dusty Reebok running shoes, and she almost cried out.

Don't, Eliza! Wait. The woman will think you're some kind of pervert. Then the toilet flushed and the plaid shorts disappeared. So did the skinny legs.

"Melody!" Eliza yelled. "Wait! Please wait!" She tried to hurry, but nylon briefs don't unroll quickly against a sweaty stomach. Eliza dashed out of the cubicle zipping her pants. By the time she got to the door, the plaid shorts were rounding the curve where the path led into a pine thicket. Still yelling, Eliza ran after them.

She was just in time to see the woman leave the trail and veer off into trees. Eliza stumbled along behind her. "Melody, don't run away. It's Eliza!" Damn it, she knows who I am! Why doesn't she stop? Then the running woman turned and looked over her shoulder. It was only for a second, but it was long enough for Eliza to get a look at her profile. The girl was terrified. And she was Melody.

Eliza was surprised when a drop of rain plopped on her hand and thunder banged overhead. She hadn't even noticed it turning darker. Everyone was leaving the park. People swarmed into the parking lot, cramming sports equipment, picnic baskets and dirty children into cars. Eliza smelled honeysuckle as she ran past a vine wrapped around a dead tree, then fell sprawling over one of its tendrils. By the time she picked herself up, the purple plaid jogger was nowhere in sight.

She couldn't have gone far, Eliza thought. She couldn't just disappear. But this was Melody, she reminded herself. Melody was experienced at disappearing. Where could she have gone?

Eliza ran into the clearing where the young people had been playing ball just a short while before, but nothing moved there except for an empty paper sack blowing across the grass.

Brenda Grayson had seen a woman who resembled Melody leaving the park on foot. That had to be where she'd gone—unless she planned to hide here in the trees and get soaked. If she hurried, Eliza thought, maybe she could overtake her between the park and wherever the woman was going.

By the time Eliza reached the place where she'd left her car, rain splashed into puddles, drilled into her skin, and the whole area looked as if it were washed in gray. She didn't have a dry thread on her, but if she could catch up with the girl in the plaid shorts, Eliza wouldn't care.

Only a few vehicles remained in the graveled section where Eliza had parked her car. It was a dark red car. She had chosen red on purpose because it was easy to see on a lot. Only this time, it was easy to see it wasn't there. Eliza was sure she had parked it near that big oak so it wouldn't get so hot in the sun. Now the branches of the huge tree writhed in the gusting rain, and her parking space was vacant.

That was when she saw the man watching her from a few feet back on the trail.

CHAPTER EIGHTEEN

There had to be a telephone somewhere, but the man in the dark parka was blocking the way, and Eliza didn't like the looks of him. She glanced about. At the far end of the lot a few stragglers remained. "Hey! Wait a minute, I need a ride!" Eliza waved at the group of ballplayers who scampered onto a blue and white bus, then watched helplessly as they splashed away, leaving her behind. The last thing she saw was the gold lettered sign reading *Helping Hands Baptist Church.*

Probably scared them to death, Eliza thought. Or maybe they didn't see me. She rubbed her bare arms for warmth, thinking of the dry windbreaker in the trunk of her car—wherever that was.

An empty van was parked on the other side of the lot, and Eliza hid behind it while keeping an eye on the stranger on the path. Maybe he was a policeman; but why didn't he say something? She had seen two or three of them while she was walking earlier, but they wore short-sleeved khaki shirts and shorts. Where were they

153

now? There had to be some sort of headquarters, an office or something.

Eliza shivered. She had to get out of this rain. A narrow trail twisted through the underbrush behind the van, and Eliza remembered seeing a rectangular log building set back among trees on the other side of the parking lot. If she could manage to elude the watcher long enough, maybe she could work her way to it.

Eliza slid like a drunk skater on slick red mud; wet pine boughs slapped her as she ran. The man! Was the man still there? She pushed aside prickly cedar limbs to see if he was standing on the path, but her sentry had gone. *Where was he?*

Cold. Eliza felt cold inside and out. She backed against the tree, and let its fragrant branches enclose her. For a minute she felt safer here, but she couldn't stay forever. Besides, cedar made her arms itch. The rain wasn't falling as hard now beneath the trees, and Eliza saw a clear path ahead of her. What if the person watching was only a park employee, or someone looking for a ride? He hadn't said anything to threaten her. He hadn't pursued her. Had he?

The trail circled past the picnic area and the rest rooms where she had seen Melody. Eliza tucked her radio inside her shirt and walked into the clearing. The cloudburst had turned into a drizzle, but the hard red earth ran with water. At least she could get out of the weather here.

She had seen a telephone somewhere . . . and there it was—in a shelter beside the bathrooms. Eliza dug into her pocket for coins and came up with a soggy tissue. Damn! She had locked her billfold in the trunk of her car, but hadn't she read somewhere you could make an emergency call without money? Well, good time to find out. Eliza ran for the shelter, but someone else was running too. Twigs snapped behind her. Pretend it's not happening, she told herself. But the noise wouldn't go away.

Eliza looked over her shoulder. He wasn't even running: just walking fast, keeping pace with her. She couldn't see his face because of the dark parka covering the forehead and chin, but she could guess his intentions, and they weren't good.

Oh God, just get me to the phone! Get me out of here. Eliza wiped water from her face as she ran. Rain or tears? Maybe both. She couldn't even tell if she was crying. She felt like crying.

A huge puddle spread between Eliza and the telephone: too wide to jump, so she waded right through it. Her shoes and socks were so wet they sloshed when she walked, but at last the phone was there . . . in her hand. And it had a dial tone! Eliza dialed 911.

"I'm in a park—Dogwood Park," Eliza told the operator. My car is gone, and there's a man—somebody . . ." She looked behind her at the sound. The watcher in the dark parka was closing the space between them with long, businesslike strides. She could see his eyes now: dark eyes; hard eyes.

"Hurry!" Eliza screamed into the phone, then threw down the receiver and ran.

"What do you want?" she yelled back at him. *Oh, come on, Eliza! Do you really want to know?* "Go away. Leave me alone!"

There was no time to think; no time to plan the best way out. All she could do was run. Through thinning trees she saw the cabin: a small building, but large enough for an office . . . and maybe a large hulking policeman. *Please!* But the parking area was deserted and no light shone through the windows. Eliza ran up on the narrow porch leaving a trail of muddy footsteps and read the notice on the wooden door:

Park hours: 8:00 A.M.–8:00 P.M.
May–Sept.
9:00 A.M.–5:00 P.M.
Oct.–April
Trespassers will be prosecuted

Eliza threw up her hands. "Oh, prosecute me, please. Do it now." Where were the people who looked after this place? It couldn't be eight o'clock yet. If screaming and jumping up and down would have done any good, she would have shaken the place apart.

The man following her was staying out of sight, but she knew he was there. Somewhere. The only thing left to do was run for the park entrance and hope she made it. Dogwood Park was in a rural area, but the street outside was well traveled, and Eliza remembered seeing a service station about a half mile down the road. She took a deep breath, put her head down and ran.

Behind her the person in the parka ran too, now making no pretense at stealth. Why didn't he just go on and grab her? Hit her over the head? Whatever. Was he playing with her? Teasing her? *Or trying to head her off?*

Each breath cut into her chest, and she couldn't seem to get enough air. Eliza tried to listen as she ran so he wouldn't circle around and surprise her. God forbid!

What was that?

Off to the right, not too far away, she heard a wonderful sound: voices! Normal voices. Somebody laughed—a woman. Through the scrub pines, she saw them on the path above her. Eliza had forgotten about the nature trail, a meandering five-mile hike that led to a place called Red Rock Springs. Removed from the rest of the park, it was popular with couples, but she was surprised to see them there today. They must have gotten caught in the storm.

Eliza ran to meet them, waving her soaking hat in her hand. "Bob! Cindy!" she yelled. "I was worried sick! Thought you'd never come. Hurry up, will you? Mom's gonna be wondering where we are."

The first of the couples looked at her strangely and walked faster, glancing back with quick little peeks as if they were afraid they might turn to salt. But the second girl had obviously twisted her ankle, and her date walked slowly along beside her, helping her over the rocks.

Eliza grabbed his other arm. "Gosh, it's good to see

you two! I'm starving, aren't you? Wonder what's for supper." The couple in front turned and glared at her.

"Excuse me?" The girl with the lame foot drew back and stared. Her date just stared.

"Just pretend you know me, please," Eliza whispered. "I need help in the worst way! Get me out of here, and I'll explain—I promise."

Limping Foot made a terrible face as if she thought Eliza might reach out and actually touch her. She had dark, almost black hair, and the greenest eyes Eliza had ever seen. She tugged on her friend's arm in an effort to drag him away, and Eliza was afraid they would leave her there. Well, she would just have to follow them. Shove her way into the car if she had to.

But the man's eyes narrowed in concern. He wanted to smile, Eliza could tell, but he wasn't sure she was joking. Instead he put an arm around her. "By golly, I thought we'd lost you for sure, Hortense! And look at you: Bet you're colder than a banker's heart!" Together they hobbled toward the parking lot where the lone van waited.

Hortense? Eliza almost giggled, but a look from the green-eyed limper warned her against it. Was the man in the parka still behind them? She couldn't hear him near. Not until they reached the comparative safety of the van, did she dare to look back. The watcher was gone.

"Somebody took my car, and a man's been following me all over the park," Eliza told them. "If you'll just drop me off at a phone—preferably some place *dry,* I'll be forever grateful."

"Do you know who it is? Did you get a look at him?" The man who had called her Hortense threw her a wadded up beach towel.

"Come on, Charles. Let's get out of here!" his date said. "For all we know it could be an escaped lunatic."

The woman looked at Eliza. *And so could you.* She didn't say it aloud; those green eyes said it for her.

Eliza couldn't tell if they believed her or not, and she

really didn't care as long as they got her away from this park.

"You came here alone?" the other woman asked. Eliza didn't know her name. Her boyfriend just referred to her as 'Honey.' Maybe that was her name.

Eliza wrapped the towel around herself as Charles turned out of the lot, spraying water in his wake. "I was looking for somebody," she said. Not that it was any of their business, but they *were* responsible for her present status: breathing.

"Could that be your car over there?" Honey's date pointed ahead as a large blue car pulled out of a narrow side road. Eliza could make out two people inside. It wasn't the same car she and Syd had seen at Melody's apartment, but it looked like Melody inside, and she was almost certain the man behind the wheel was the one who had been following her.

"No, mine's a dark red Dodge." Eliza leaned forward and dripped on Honey's arm. "Can you make out that license?" All she could see were the last two numbers: 48.

"Too muddy," Charles said as the car ahead made a quick left turn onto the busy highway. "Boy, he's in a hurry! That the guy, you think?"

"Probably," Eliza said. "But he's gone now."

"Not necessarily, if we can phone a description in time." Charles glanced at Eliza through the rear view mirror. "You didn't leave your keys in it, did you?"

Eliza made a face. He sounded like her father. "No, but I think I know how they got in. I didn't want to be bothered with carrying keys around with me, so I used one of those magnet attachments—the kind you stick under the fender somewhere. He must've been watching . . . or it was somebody who knew I did that."

Charles drove her directly to the small yellow brick building that housed the community police. They had dispatched a car to the park in response to her emergency call, Eliza was told. They must have passed it along the way.

The girl with the green eyes (her name was Andrea, Eliza learned,) was about to have a hissy fit in her hurry to leave, but Charles and the other two didn't seem to mind when the officer asked them to stay and make a statement.

The first thing Eliza saw when they stepped inside the building was a large photograph of Melody pinned to the bulletin board. It didn't take long for the police to learn what she was doing in Dogwood Park.

"Oh, I remember reading about her!" Honey said, running fingers through her damp hair. "I'm glad they found that baby . . . she's okay, isn't she?"

"Yes, she's fine," Eliza assured her, remembering for the first time that she hadn't called home.

They sat in a row of very hard chairs in the green-tiled lobby. "Maybe something will turn up now that they have a better description of that car," Charles said. "The last two numbers on the license should give them a little more to go on."

Eliza tried to smile in reply, but all she could manage was a shiver. A policeman had brought her a man's shirt to wear, and Eliza slipped into it gratefully. She didn't care if it had a prison number stenciled on it. It was dry and warm. She peeled off her wet shoes and socks and stuffed them under the chair. "Could I make a collect call to Minerva? Somebody will have to come for me, I guess." Every parent's nightmare: *Come and get me; I'm in jail!*

Charles leaned forward. "How far is it? We might be—"

With a swift catlike motion, Andrea encircled his wrist. If her knuckles were any tighter, Eliza thought, her fingers would fall off.

"Looks like that won't be necessary." The thickset sergeant leaned over his desk. "Officer on patrol out there says there's a red Dodge parked on a side street about a half mile from Dogwood Park. Keys were under the mat."

So Melody was alive! During the long drive home, Eliza puzzled over all that had happened. She was tempted to stop at a shopping center for dry clothes and a sandwich before starting out for Minerva, but what if that same man followed her? She was afraid to stop, to get out of her car alone. She hated him for that.

Obviously the man had expected her. Eliza had been to the park twice before: once with Dorcas and the last time with Sydney. He knew where she put her car keys, and he wanted her there alone. For what? It looked as if the two of them had planned to get her into that car and take her away. She would just disappear. Like Melody.

The lights of home had never looked as welcoming. The two of them waited on the porch, Ben Figg and Olivia. Family. Or trying hard to be. "Eliza, you're soaked to the skin—and look at you, barefooted as a yard dog." Ben Figg hugged her close. "Come and get something to eat. Livvy's been keeping it warm."

Eliza hugged him back. What the heck, she hugged them both. "In a minute. Just let me get on dry clothes."

Mattie was in her crib sleeping. Her little chest moved up and down as it should, and now and then she made those funny swimming motions. Good. Part of the rock that had settled in Eliza's stomach dissolved, and she grabbed a robe from her closet and headed for the shower.

When the telephone rang, Eliza snatched it quickly before it could wake Mattie.

"I want to see my baby," Melody Lamb said.

Chapter Nineteen

"Eliza, are you sure it was Melody?" Her dad slid a steaming bowl of canned tomato soup in front of her, and Eliza absently crumbled a cracker into it.

"It sounded like her—just like her." She stirred the cracker into orange mush.

Ben Figg paced the kitchen. He had put in at least a mile already. "It could've been a tape . . . a tape of Melody's voice."

"Why play a tape of her voice when they've got the real thing?" Eliza asked. When nobody answered, she found them avoiding her eyes. "Oh," she said. "You mean . . . you think . . ."

"What else did she say?" her dad asked.

"Nothing. I hung up." Eliza rubbed her hands together. They still felt numb. The shock of hearing that voice had run like cold water all the way down her arm and into her chest. She had wanted to throw the receiver across the room. "It *was* Melody. I saw her."

Olivia put a bowl of salad on the table. "Maybe she'll call back."

"I hope not," Eliza said. "Oh, Lord, I hope not. Why is she doing this to me—to us? What does she want?"

"Sounds as if she wants Mattie," Ben said. "Or somebody does."

"Well, she can't have her. Not if I can help it. I think the woman's gone crazy. Why else would she do something like this?" Eliza put her head in her hands. She ached all over, but she would sit up all night if she had to; sit by Mattie's bed and watch over her. She wouldn't close her eyes.

Someone was rubbing her back, kneading her shoulders. Her father. "Eat your soup and go to bed. We won't let anything happen to that baby."

Eliza was tempted. She swallowed a spoonful of soup: salty and hot—just what she wanted. "Kemper should be in on this," she told them. "I guess we'd better call the police."

She would have to answer questions, and she felt like a lump of modeling clay. Eliza sat in the most uncomfortable chair she could find to wait for Kemper Mungo. She had to stay awake.

This time he came with Chief Asbury who looked almost as tired as Eliza felt, and he wasn't in the best of moods. "Coulda been anybody," he said. "Lots of crazies out there get a kick out of this kind of thing." The chief wiggled his mouth all around as if he were trying to scratch his nose without using his hands. Eliza watched, fascinated. Did he know how silly he looked when he did that?

She told him about seeing Melody, or a woman who looked like Melody, in Dogwood Park.

"And where were the park police all this time? Should've been somebody on duty there." The chief nodded curtly to Kemper who pulled a small notebook from his pocket.

"Doesn't make sense them just going off and leaving the place unattended," he added.

"Somebody called them," Eliza said. "Told them a

child was lost on the other side of the park, way up there near the springs."

Kemper frowned. "And was there?"

"No. It was just a distraction to get them out of the way," Eliza said. "They told me about it at the police station later. Said they never did find anybody up there."

"Did they say who called?" Chief Asbury finally rubbed his nose. Thank goodness. "Man or woman?"

"It was a woman." Eliza yawned in spite of herself. "Probably Melody. After the man started following me, I didn't see her again."

The chief took out a large white handkerchief and blew. "You're sure this was Melody you saw?"

Eliza stared at him until he finally looked away. If one more person asked her that, she would say something so awful her father would disown her, and she wouldn't apologize for it either.

"Well, by God, if she comes there again, we'll be ready for her." The chief slapped his leg. "I'll get in touch with the precinct there tonight." He said this more to Ben than Eliza, as if her father were the one who had slid around all afternoon in the mud and slop. "And you might want to get a tracer on that phone. If she calls back, at least we'll know where she's calling from."

Chief Asbury looked at Eliza as if he had just remembered she was there, and she wasn't sure, but she thought he was trying to smile. "Now, don't you worry, little lady. We're going to put an end to this business once and for all." He shook his head. "I'll get to the bottom of this come hell or high water!"

Eliza glanced at Kemper but he wouldn't look at her. As tired and as worried as she was, she had to hold her breath to keep from laughing. Chief Milton Asbury was going to look after things, by golly! They could all sleep better tonight.

"I'm taking Mattie to work with me," Eliza said the next morning at breakfast. She looked across the table at

Ben who was slicing a peach into his cereal. "Would you put her playpen in the trunk of my car?"

"Don't be ridiculous," he said. "I'm perfectly capable of looking after Mattie. Nothing will happen, I promise. Besides, Dorcas Youngblood's right next door. The two of us can handle things, don't worry."

"What if she calls again?"

Her dad slammed bread into the toaster. "Then I'll pick up the phone and say, 'Hello.' "

Eliza spooned cereal into the baby's mouth and gave Ben Figg a look.

"They're putting that tracing gadget on the phone today, aren't they?" Olivia exercised with waist twists while waiting for the kettle to boil. "If she does call, at least we'll know where she is.

"Oh, and by the way, speaking of calls, some girl phoned here yesterday asking for you. Called twice, as a matter of fact."

"What girl? It wasn't—"

"No, not Melody! She gave me her name . . . Penny something. Seemed a bit intense to me," Olivia said. "I promised I'd have you return her call, but in the excitement over Melody I forgot all about it."

"That's okay. I'll phone her when I get to Bellawood. Besides, if it was all that important, seems she would've called back."

"Livvy has to get on back," Ben said as his wife left the room, "but I don't feel right about going just yet. Besides, I want to talk with Milt Asbury before I leave, find out if he's heard anything."

"Oh, I expect the chief has the case solved by now." Eliza resisted a giggle. "Or by noon at least.

"But if Olivia takes the car, how will you get back to Atlanta?"

"C. C. and Frances Reece have tickets to Theatre of the Stars. I'll grab a ride with them after you get home from work."

Eliza didn't argue. Mattie would probably be fine with

Dorcas, but she felt assured just knowing her father would be in the house all day.

Eliza turned to find Olivia standing in the doorway, purse under her arm. "Can I do anything for anyone before I go?" she asked.

She had already eaten her little cup of fruit yogurt, stripped the sheets from their bed, showered, and ironed her blue-striped shirtwaist; and now she stood wrinkle-free and rosebud-fresh before them. Olivia had more energy than a kitten, and Eliza was amazed there was enough of her left to cast a shadow.

"Sit down and have another cup of tea," Eliza said, delegating baby face-wiping chores to her dad. "There's a picture I've been meaning to have framed. Won't take me a minute to get it."

She found the watercolor of pastel iris in the back of Melody's closet where it had been since January and took it down to the kitchen.

"That's lovely." Olivia stood to see it better. "What delicate shades of lavender . . . almost an orchid. Who painted it?"

"Melody's mother. Her natural mother. It's the only thing she had of hers. When she tried to hang it, it slipped from her hands and chipped the frame; glass has a little crack in it too. I wanted to get it framed for the baby— maybe have it matted. What do you think?"

"For that front room upstairs? Oh yes! Ben, I've seen just the thing." Olivia turned the picture over. "Let's get it out of this old broken frame before it cuts somebody. One of those large manilla envelopes should do for now."

Eliza shoved the trash can under the table to collect the debris. Whoever framed the painting had cut cardboard from a Belk's box to use for a backing and the corners were creased and frayed.

"Wait a minute," Ben said. "Don't throw that away. There's something underneath—a photograph or something." His long fingers rescued the faded color photograph before it got tossed away.

Everyone ignored the watercolor as Olivia placed the other picture in the center of the table. It was a studio portrait of two little girls, and they looked just alike.

"Twins," Eliza said, taking a closer look. They seemed to be about two years old.

Ben Figg frowned at the photograph, then picked it up and took it to the window. "Melody," he said. "They look something like Melody did when she came here; younger, of course, but she had that look about her."

"She was how old then?" Olivia said. "Five? Six?"

"Five," Ben told her. "Had a birthday that summer."

"Maybe Melody had sisters," Eliza suggested. "They could've been her sisters."

But her father shook his head. "No, it's Melody all right. Says so right here. Look." He turned the portrait over for them to see the faint handwriting penciled on the back: *Melody and Marilyn Gaines, Adam's Ford, N.C., 1974.*

"Well, Tootie Squat," Ben Figg said, scooping Mattie from her chair. "What do you think about that?"

"That explains it," Eliza said as they sat on the back porch after her father left that night. "It was Melody's twin we saw. Had to be."

"Then where's Melody?" Syd asked. She propped her big feet on the rough bench Martha Figg always used for a plant stand, and scraped the last molecule of peach ice cream from her bowl. "Lord, that was good! My stomach thinks it's died and gone to heaven."

"Have some more," Dorcas offered. She had brought over a container left from Minerva's Fourth of July celebration, along with a plateful of brownies.

"Well, maybe just a smidgen," Sydney said. "This doesn't have any calories, does it?"

Dorcas laughed. "Oh, they melt in your stomach,

didn't you know that?" She turned to Eliza. "Do you think Melody knew she had a twin?"

"Don't ask me what Melody knew! I haven't figured her out. But what is Melody's twin doing at Dogwood Park? What does she want with me?"

Syd looked up. "Are you sure it's her twin you saw?"

Eliza moaned. "We're beginning to sound like those comedians from the old movies: 'Who's on first?' I'm not even sure of my own name anymore."

"Modine," Syd told her. "Modine Gunch."

Eliza started to laugh, then stood suddenly. "What was that? Did you hear Mattie crying?"

"Relax, it's a cat; see it over there next to the woodpile?" Syd gently pushed her back into the chair. "Mattie's asleep. She's fine, just like she was fifteen minutes ago."

"She wants Mattie, you know," Eliza said.

Dorcas stopped rocking. "Who, sugar? Who wants Mattie?"

"Melody . . . Marilyn . . . whoever!"

"Did she call again today?" Syd asked.

"No, but she will," Eliza said. "I know she will. And I'll be ready when she does."

Sydney put down her bowl and looked at her. "Meaning what?"

"I've got to find out where she is. Where she came from," Eliza said. "Does anybody know how far it is to Adam's Ford, North Carolina?"

CHAPTER TWENTY

"What in the world is the matter with Penny Shilling-law's mother?" Eliza asked her neighbor the next morning.

Dorcas looked up from her log cabin quilting squares. "What do you mean?"

"I tried to return Penny's call a couple of times yesterday, and her mother acted like I was after the family silver or something. The woman was barely civil, told me Penny wasn't there. She was there all right! She just wasn't getting the message."

Dorcas squinted as she threaded a needle. "McIver," she said.

"What?"

"Penny's mother. Darlene Shillinglaw was a McIver. All those McIvers are queer . . . Oh, not *that* kind of queer! Just peculiar. My nephew went to school with her brother Harold; Luke said he ate the same thing for lunch every day and hummed under his breath in class. Drove the teachers crazy."

169

"Well, something's wrong there," Eliza said. "When I telephoned a few minutes ago, Penny's mother snatched the phone before it finished the first ring, practically screamed at me. 'I *told* you Penny's not here!' she said. 'She's staying with relatives for a while, and I don't know when she'll be back.' "

"Not with Harold, I hope," Dorcas said.

"The nasty woman hung up on me. What's she so upset about? What did I do?"

"Well, for one thing you cast suspicion on her daughter. I don't think you'll be on her Christmas list this year."

Eliza poured formula into a bottle for Mattie. "I still think that girl knows something. That must've been why she called—only her mother doesn't want her to tell me. Why?"

Dorcas shrugged. "McIver," she said.

Eliza went to work, but her heart stayed on Habersham Street. She called so many times to check on Mattie, Dorcas got downright surly.

"Chinese laundry," she answered in what she thought was a foreign accent when Eliza phoned for the fourth time.

"That's not funny, Dorcas. Minerva doesn't even have a Chinese laundry. How's Mattie? Has Melody called again?"

"Mattie's fine—or was until you woke her. And no, Melody hasn't called. How could she with you tying up the line? Now get off the phone, Eliza. I have other things to do."

"If you don't want me to call, just say so, Dorcas. No need to be wishy-washy."

Eliza saw Kemper Mungo pulling into the parking lot as she hung up the phone, and went outside to meet him.

"Any more calls?" Kemper fanned with his hat as they sat in the gray shade of Bellawood's sprawling porch. It was July in Georgia and it felt like it.

Eliza shook her head. "Not yet, but she will. If it's Melody, and I'm pretty sure it is, she won't give up on that baby."

"How can you be so sure it's Melody? Maybe it's her twin."

"But why would she be interested in Mattie?" Eliza asked.

"That still doesn't explain why she'd walk off and leave her, then pull this on-again-off-again act," Kemper said. "If Melody wants her baby back, why doesn't she just come and get her?"

Eliza watched an ant zigzagging across the floor. What if she did? What could she, Eliza, do if Melody showed up and demanded Mattie? "What about her twin?" she asked. "Did you find out anything about the family? Are there still Gaineses in that town in North Carolina?"

"Adam's Ford. No immediate family, or none that we could find. The twins were born there twenty-two years ago to . . . just a minute, I wrote it down . . ." Kemper took a folded sheet of yellow notepaper from his shirt pocket and shook it open.

". . . Lynda Dawson Gaines and Robert Troy Gaines." He looked up briefly. "Melody's daddy was a truck driver, died when the twins were about a year and a half from injuries received in an accident, they said. Their mama moved away soon after that."

"Moved where?"

Kemper stuffed the paper back into his pocket. "Nobody seems to know. Had to talk to three or four people at the police station there before I even found anybody who remembered them."

Eliza frowned. "Adam's Ford. Never heard of it before now; how big a town is it, do you think?"

"'Bout three or four thousand I guess. Drove through there once on the way to Raleigh. Not much to it."

"Sounds like the family's been gone twenty years at least," Eliza said. "Wonder what happened to the twins' mother?"

Eliza stood as a tour bus pulled into the circular drive

and stopped at the foot of the steps. "Gotta go, we're short on volunteers today and I promised to help in the gift shop." She paused at the door. "Did you have a chance to talk with anybody else in Adam's Ford?"

"Just the police—and a clerk at the county seat. Had to go through the Department of Records there to find out about the twins' birth." He stood aside for a covey of middle-aged sightseers. "Why?"

"Maybe they still have kinfolks there . . . a cousin or something. How far is this place?"

"Farther than you need to go," Kemper said as he started down the old brick walk. "Just leave this thing to us, Eliza. Stay out of it." He said something else but Eliza didn't hear him because a large woman in a violent purple blouse demanded to know where the rest room was.

Were Melody and her twin sister involved in some kind of scheme? Ben Figg said Melody was placed in a foster home as a toddler, and Eliza had never heard her mention having a sister. If the people at Social Services knew there was a twin, surely they would have kept the two of them together. Why were the two girls separated, and how did they find one another after all this time?

Eliza rang up a corn-shuck doll and a jar of sorghum syrup for a customer. She wasn't sure how Marilyn figured in this, but she felt certain Melody was still alive, and in typical Melody fashion, she was using Eliza to get what she wanted. This time it was Mattie.

Only a great fear of Dorcas Youngblood kept Eliza from calling home again. She didn't think Melody or her twin would try anything during the day, and the police were keeping an eye on the house, but they couldn't be there every minute.

Mattie would be napping now, and Dorcas probably was watching her afternoon soaps. She wouldn't even talk if you called during her favorites, and Eliza realized her neighbor's agreeing to babysit was the ultimate concession. But this was different. This was war, and for the next few nights Dorcas would be staying in Melody's room upstairs. "I'll feel better if you aren't alone," she said. "But don't you worry," her neighbor assured her. "Nobody's getting past Dorcas Youngblood!"

Uh-huh, sure, Eliza thought. If anyone did approach Mattie, Dorcas could stab them with her sewing needle, while she—Eliza—bashed them over the head with her unfinished dissertation. Oh, what was she going to do about Mattie?

If only Melody would telephone, the phone company would be able to trace the call—and eventually Melody. At least they would know where she was. But Melody didn't call that night or the next. Did she know about the tracer they had put on the telephone? Maybe she wouldn't call again. Then what?

A couple of days later, tiring of taking sandwiches to work, Eliza came home to a late lunch of shrimp salad and fresh tomatoes. Dorcas had just put Mattie down for her nap, and the two of them were sitting down to eat when the telephone rang.

Dorcas put down her fork and tossed her napkin aside. "I'll get it."

Eliza looked up from her iced tea to find her neighbor standing in the doorway with a dazed look on her face and the receiver in her hand.

"It's Melody," Dorcas mouthed silently. She thrust the receiver away from her as though it might bite.

"Who are you, and what do you want?" Eliza still held the glass of tea. It smelled of lemon and mint.

"You know who I am, Eliza. I want my baby. I want Mattie."

"Very well, come and get her." Eliza gripped the phone. *Fat chance,* she thought.

"I can't do that right now. Look, why can't we meet somewhere?"

Eliza held her breath to listen better. The woman did sound like Melody. "What about tonight at that rest stop just outside of town? After dark—about nine?" she said.

"You've got to be kidding! I'm not taking that baby

anywhere to meet you, wherever you are. Not tonight, or any other night! If you really want to see Mattie, you'll have to come here." Eliza's hand shook as she hung up the phone.

"Well? Dorcas hovered over her. "What do we do now?"

"We find out where she's calling from," Eliza said, dialing the number the phone company had given her. The process took only a few minutes, but it seemed to Eliza they waited hours before someone called them back.

Dorcas stood with pencil poised as Eliza picked up the phone. "Well?" she said. "Where is she?"

"At a pay phone in front of the Texaco station . . . about five blocks from here!"

But there was no sign of the elusive Melody by the time Oscar Watts got there in his patrol car. Well, really, Eliza didn't expect her to be there waiting.

"She knows I'm here. She must have been watching when I came home for lunch," Eliza said. "We've got to find this crackpot, whoever she is, before she gets any closer!" She looked at her neighbor across their untouched plates. "I'm scared, Dorcas. Scared for Mattie. She's not safe here. Where are we going to hide her?"

"She's not only getting closer, she's getting careless," Dorcas said. "Don't worry, they'll find her now—and soon."

"Maybe even sooner if we help things along," Eliza said. "I'm going to Adam's Ford as early as I can get away tomorrow, and I want you to promise me you won't tell Kemper Mungo."

"Tell him, nothing!" Dorcas said. "I'm going with you."

By the time they worked out the details, Eliza felt like a character in a spy novel. Sydney would keep Mattie until they got back. "Oh, don't worry," she said. "I'll just smear a little dirt on her and she'll blend right in with my brood." More seriously, she added, "I won't take my eyes from her, I promise. But what if Melody calls while you and Dorcas are gone?''

''Dad's staying overnight to answer the phone—just in case. He and C. C. Reece have to tie up some loose ends about selling the hardware store, and I told him this would be a little vacation for Dorcas and me.''

''You mean he doesn't know where you're going?''

Eliza shrugged. ''Not exactly. And we're leaving my car there too. Dorcas will sneak Mattie out the back way and leave her with you, then pick me up at Bellawood in her car. I'd like to get a head start before anyone knows we're gone.''

''Well, if they can figure all that out, they're a lot smarter than I am,'' Syd admitted. ''Seems like you have it covered, but do be careful, Eliza. We don't know who we're dealing with here, but whoever it is, she's nuts.''

Eliza mingled with a bus load of tourists as she waited for Dorcas that afternoon in Bellawood's steamy parking lot. The air conditioning was like a winter kiss as she slid into the seat beside her.

Eliza let the coolness caress her damp face. ''Whew! At last! Did everything go okay?''

''Far as I know.'' Dorcas scattered gravel as she pulled out of the drive. ''This is kind of fun! I feel like Agent Double Oh Seven . . . Oh, and some man came by as I was getting ready to leave. Thought I'd never get rid of him.''

''What man? What did he want?''

''You, I imagine. At least, that's what he said.'' Her neighbor turned down a side road. ''Said his name was Charles something or other. Brought back your radio.''

Charles? Eliza didn't know any Charles. Did she? ''What radio?''

''That little bitty thing you use with the earphones. Said you left it in his van at Dogwood Park.''

''You didn't tell him where we were going, did you?'' Eliza said.

Dorcas just looked at her. "I didn't even tell him where you worked, but he insisted on giving me his phone number, so I said I'd pass it along. I think he wants you to call him."

Charles. Eliza didn't even know his last name, but he had rescued her from the phantom of Dogwood Park. Still, she didn't know anything else about him. How had he known where to find her?

CHAPTER TWENTY-ONE

"Kemper was right," Eliza said as they parked in front of Grindstaff & Son's Groceries & Sundries. "There isn't much to Adam's Ford." Behind a fly-speckled window, dust collected on a pyramid of canned goods, and the once-red sign over the door hung at a dangerous tilt.

Mr. Grindstaff—or maybe it was his son—a balding red-faced man, remembered Lynda Gaines and her twin daughters, but he didn't know where she went after her husband was killed. "You might ask J. D. down at *The Messenger*," he told Eliza as she paid for a Nugrape soda. "I reckon he's got papers going clear back to that other Adam!" The grocer pointed to a small brick building on the other side of the street. "Yeah, he's there—door's open."

Eliza thanked him and hurried across the road.

J. D., she found to her surprise, was not much older than she and had been in Adam's Ford only a few years. He did, however, offer to let Eliza and her friend browse through dog eared issues of *The Messenger* that did, indeed, appear to go back to the original Adam.

An hour later, ink-smeared and dusty, Dorcas shoved back her cane-bottomed chair and stretched. "I give up! It's like the woman never existed. Are you sure we're in the right town?"

"With twin babies, I guess she must've been too busy for an active social life," Eliza said. "The only thing I know about Lynda Gaines is that she painted that watercolor."

J. D. turned from the paste-up table behind them. "Maybe somebody in the Arts Council would know her."

"Arts Council? Adam's Ford has an Arts Council?" Eliza tried not to sound surprised—although she was, and a little jealous too. Minerva didn't have an Arts Council.

"Well, it's county wide," the editor said, "but we have a couple of representatives. Ferg McMasters works in Raleigh, but Liz Bartholomew might know. Retired teacher —lives about three blocks over on May Apple Street." He reached for the phone. "Here, I'll give her a call, see if she's home."

"Why, of course I remember Lynda Gaines!" the woman in the straw hat said. Liz Bartholomew had just come from her garden with a huge basket of tomatoes, and she kicked off her muddy shoes at the back door. "Here, come on in and I'll fix us a glass of tea. Looks like it's going to be another hot one, doesn't it?" She held the screen door for them, and Eliza and Dorcas trotted in obediently.

"It was sad about that young woman. Had something wrong with her heart, I think . . . and so talented too." With her floppy hat Liz Bartholomew fanned a strand of gray hair from her face and led them into a shadowy dining room. "I have one of hers right over my buffet: 'Hydrangea in a White Pitcher.' Beautiful, isn't it? Nobody could paint flowers like Lynda."

The painting was beautiful, and Eliza didn't have to

pretend to admire it. There was no doubt of the woman's talent. "What happened to her? Where did she go from here?"

Their hostess moved into the kitchen and clinked ice into tall green glasses. "Heard she ended up in Georgia somewhere. Didn't live too long after Bobby was killed . . . and those girls just babies."

"Do you know where they are now?" Dorcas accepted a glass of tea. "Were there relatives?"

"Just a cousin, at least that's the only one I know of. Jimmie Lee. Jimmie Lee Pringle. Lives out toward Sanford in one of those trailer parks, only they want you to call them mobile homes now." The older woman rattled the ice in her glass and drained the last swallow. "Don't think the two of them got along so well, from what I was able to tell."

Oh Lord, Eliza thought with a look at Dorcas. They were going to have trouble with that one, she just knew it!

And she was right.

A possum. If a possum could turn into a woman, it would look exactly like Jimmie Lee Pringle. Her short brownish-gray hair stuck up just as a possum's did, and she had a sharp, pointed nose and beady eyes. The woman stood in the doorway with one arm, like an iron bar, across it. Behind her Eliza heard a television game show: one of the sillier ones whose contestants didn't seem to have any raising at all.

"Yes, Lynda Gaines was my cousin," she said, obviously impatient to get back to her program. "Died a long time ago. Why?" Her eyes brightened. "She didn't leave a will or something, did she? Sometimes you hear about people who—"

Eliza was pleased to disappoint her. "I'm afraid not. We're trying to find out what happened to her daughters."

"Oh yeah, the twins. A couple in Raleigh raised one of them. He had some sort of government job I think."

"One of them? Do you remember which one?" A tempting stream of cool air escaped from the crack in the door and came within breathing distance of Eliza's hot face, but Jimmie Lee wasn't sharing it. She stepped quickly onto the simmering deck and pulled the door shut behind her. Eliza hoped she'd locked herself out.

"Never could tell those two apart," the woman said. "Reckon Lynda kind of expected me to take them, but I couldn't on account of my nerves. Just shot to pieces, don't you know? And *two* of them. Well, I just couldn't deal with the noise . . ."

Behind her the television rose to a boisterous crescendo. Eliza avoided her friend's eyes. "Would you happen to have the family's address?" she asked. "It's really important that we find her . . . I'm not sure, but there could be money in it . . . maybe somewhere down the line."

She heard Dorcas gasp.

"Well, I'll look. Know I've got it written down somewhere. Lynda sent Christmas cards for a while after she left here. Didn't live too long, don't you know? But she wrote me about those people—seems like it was somebody she'd known before."

Eliza stepped into the shade of a pine tree to wait for the woman's return, while Dorcas, declaring she wasn't going to be an accomplice to deceit, waited in her air-conditioned car.

"Copied this down for you," Jimmie Lee said, returning with a small piece of notepaper. "Been close to twenty years, now, so these people might've moved." She hesitated as if she wasn't sure it was in her best interest to give Eliza the address. "You will let me know, won't you? Not that I care about the money, but I'd kinda like to keep in touch with those girls. After all, they are family, and I reckon I'm about the only kin they got."

* * *

Velma Rogers lived in a small, neat house on the outskirts of Raleigh: the same house where the Rogerses had
taken Melody's twin sister to raise nineteen years before.
She had sounded tired, and a little sad, Eliza thought,
when she telephoned her earlier to explain why they
were coming. Impulsively, Eliza had bought flowers from
an outdoor market. "She just sounds like she could use
some," she admitted to Dorcas.

On the drive over, Eliza sat clutching them in her lap,
dreading to hear what Velma Rogers might tell them.
Why would Lynda Gaines find a home here for one twin,
but not the other? Surely there were childless couples
willing—even eager—to adopt the two sisters. "They
were pretty children, and not much more than babies,"
Eliza said as she and Dorcas walked the short path to the
door. "Why separate them?"

"Maybe the mother hoped to be able to keep one—at
least for a time," Dorcas said. "Or maybe this family
wouldn't—or couldn't—accept them both."

But Velma Rogers told another story. They sat on a
green brocaded sofa in the dim living room while Eliza
told her about Melody. "I don't understand why they
didn't keep them together," she said.

"They were such dainty little girls," the woman said.
"Precious-looking children, and Henry and I did offer to
take them both, but Lynda thought they'd be happier
apart." She hurried off to find a vase for the flowers, but
not before Eliza noticed her eyes. The sadness was there,
and something else as well.

"I wonder why?" Eliza said when the woman returned.
"I think Melody would've liked knowing she had a sister.
She seemed so lonely sometimes; everybody needs a
family."

To her surprise, Velma sank into the chair across from
her and sighed. Finally she shook her head and looked up
at them. There were tears in her eyes. "Not always," she
said. "In this case, I think their mother made the right
decision. Marilyn had emotional problems, you see. She

was a difficult child. And unhappy, so unhappy! It hasn't been easy."

Marilyn had been strong willed and destructive as a little girl, Velma Rogers told them. "She had a cruel streak—even as a tiny little thing. I think her mother must have realized it. Why once, I even caught her trying to throw the neighbor's cat in the lily pool. Henry and I . . . well, we were afraid to have pets. We were hoping she'd grow out of it, but of course she didn't."

The Rogerses didn't realize the extent of her problems until Marilyn reached junior high age. "We found out she'd been experimenting with drugs, and drinking, of course. We worried that she might be sexually active as well, but she claimed not, and I tended to believe her. Marilyn wasn't a giving person—though that might have come later. By the time she got out of high school, she'd exhausted most of our savings and all of our patience." The frail woman placed both hands firmly on her lap. "To tell you the truth, at that point I didn't care!

"And Henry . . . well, my husband wasn't strong, and his heart finally gave out on him. He died almost two years ago." Her voice grew louder. "I have no doubt that all that trouble with Marilyn hastened him to his grave. He loved her, you know, even with all her problems. He never gave up hoping."

"What happened to her?" Dorcas asked.

"Left here right before her twentieth birthday," Velma said with resignation in her voice. "We'd tried everything: therapy, counseling—even sent her off to college for a while. Wouldn't go to class, and they finally expelled her." Velma leaned back in her rose-flowered wing chair and seemed to study the placid lake scene over the mantel. "Last I heard was about a year ago when she called wanting money. Said she was married and living somewhere in Georgia . . . didn't even ask about her father. Didn't care, I guess." Velma took a tissue from her pocket and wiped her eyes. "But I told her! I told her Henry was dead, and then I hung up on her. It was the hardest thing I ever had to do—like throwing your own child away."

Eliza groped for the packet of tissues in her purse. Her throat felt salty and hot. Dorcas cleared her throat and blinked. "I'm sorry, so sorry," Eliza said. "But that explains a lot. We're trying to find Marilyn; I can't tell you how important it is." She reached out for the woman's small hand. "Mrs. Rogers, can you tell us where she is?"

Velma Rogers sat straighter, and her eyes were no longer wet. "Yes, I can tell you where she is. Marilyn is dead. Dead and buried, and I didn't even go to the funeral."

This couldn't be happening. "When?" Eliza asked. "When did she die?"

The woman looked calmly into her lap. "It was the end of June—the twenty-second, to be exact. Her husband called to tell me: Arnold, his name was—Arnold Blodgett." She shrugged. "I couldn't feel anything; not sorrow —not even relief, only numbness. They buried her the next day."

One look at Dorcas told Eliza they were thinking the same thing. *June the twenty-second was the day after Melody disappeared.* "Are you sure it was Marilyn they buried?" she asked.

"What do you mean? Oh, dear God . . . I never thought . . ." Velma looked longingly at the lake painting as if she might walk quietly into it.

"Do you remember where she's buried?" Dorcas asked.

"Somewhere in Georgia. I'd never heard of the town. It's not too far from Atlanta, this Arnold said. They buried her there." Velma stood and went to the mantel. "Now maybe she's at peace."

Dorcas rose and stood beside her. "Mrs. Rogers, Marilyn didn't . . . well, she didn't take her own life?"

"Oh, no! My goodness, no. Marilyn would never do that. It was an accident. Marilyn was taking a bath, you see, and the radio fell into the tub."

Eliza had never considered a bathtub as a dangerous weapon, but apparently this Arnold did. "If we looked at a map of Georgia, do you think you'd remember the town?"

"Yes, I think so," Velma said. "Seems it began with a C."

Eliza walked about the yard with Velma Rogers while Dorcas went to the car for the map. Henry had planted these roses, she said, and now that he was gone, she spent much of her time taking care of them—like a part of him they were.

Eliza sniffed a yellow blossom. She didn't have the heart to tell this kind lady her daughter might have been murdered. Or was it her daughter? She had to find out who was buried in Marilyn's grave.

CHAPTER TWENTY-TWO

V elma ran a finger down the list of Georgia towns. "Cedartown—no. Covington—not quite right . . . wait a minute, I missed one. Here it is: Carrollton. That's where they lived—Carrollton."

"That would be about right," Eliza said, looking at the map. "It's west of Atlanta, not too far from Dogwood Park. Are you sure that's the place?"

"As sure as I can be of anything at my age," Velma said. "I suppose we could call the funeral director there and see if they were in charge of the service—if there was a service. Marilyn probably wouldn't have cared one way or the other."

It took two phone calls to find them, but Hemphill Brothers Mortuary said they had buried Mrs. Blodgett in Orchard Valley Cemetery on the twenty-third of June.

And didn't wait long about it, either, Eliza thought.

It was late afternoon when Velma Rogers walked with them to the car. She seemed to want to talk about Marilyn; it was as if they had triggered a release mechanism

185

by being there, and the woman's stymied emotions rushed out.

Lynda Gaines had become friends with the Rogerses as a young girl when Velma taught at the local high school, she told them. They had kept in touch, and when Lynda realized she might not have long to live, she remembered the childless couple who had always wanted a family of their own.

"Lynda was frail, even as a girl," Velma said. "But she didn't learn of her heart defect until her pregnancy with the twins. It got progressively worse, and after her husband was killed, she knew she wouldn't be able to raise them. 'I want to know my girls will be taken care of,' she told us." Velma pressed her hands to her face. "I don't know why she chose us for Marilyn."

"Probably because you were patient," Dorcas said.

"And loving," Eliza added. "But it looks like her health gave out on her before she could find a place for Melody. The child went from one foster home to another before she was finally adopted. I don't know how many places she lived before she came to us."

"But Melody wasn't a problem," Dorcas reminded her. "From what I remember, she was well behaved. Almost too quiet. Her mother probably thought she would have an easier time of it."

"I'm sure Melody wasn't aware she had a sister," Eliza said. "Has Marilyn always known?"

"Oh, no! There were times I wanted to tell her, but Lynda made us promise to wait. 'Let her grow up an individual,' she said. 'There'll be time enough when they're grown.' Henry and I had planned to tell her when she was twenty-one, but she found out for herself."

"When? Do you remember?" Eliza stopped with her hand on the car door.

"She was around sixteen or so, I think. Needed her birth certificate for something or other—a job maybe or driver's license—can't remember what. It said on the birth certificate that she was a twin." Velma Rogers looked grim. "Marilyn was furious with Henry and me for not telling her, wouldn't believe I didn't know where her sister was."

"Wonder how she found her?" Dorcas said.

"Bullied me until I gave her the few letters we'd had from her mother after she left here. They were postmarked from somewhere in Georgia—not Carrollton. Seems like it was on the other side of the state. Eventually, I thought she'd forgotten about it, but she must've kept those old letters, traced her sister from there."

And I know when she found her, Eliza thought as they said good-bye.

"I wonder where Arnold was when the radio *fell* into the bathtub," Eliza said as they crept through Raleigh's rush hour traffic.

"Arnold?" Dorcas glared at the motorist who cut into her lane.

"Arnold Blodgett, Marilyn's husband. I have a feeling he's the same man who turned that dog loose on Melody and killed poor Jessie Gilreath."

Dorcas made a face. "So it's *poor* Jessie now? Thought you couldn't stand her."

"Well, I can't. Couldn't, but she's dead now, so I don't have to." That sounded awful. "For heaven's sake, Dorcas, the woman didn't deserve that. Why do you have to pick everything apart?"

"I've taken on Jessie's duties as your nosy neighbor, and that's what we do best."

"Well, pick out a phone booth, will you? I want to call Syd, see if Mattie's okay."

"Shoot, you've missed it!" Syd said when she came to the phone.

"Missed what? What do you mean?"

"What a kid! That Mattie learned to walk, talk and work advanced trigonometry since you called me this morning. She's in there now reading Gibbon's *Decline and Fall of the Roman Empire.*"

"She read that last week," Eliza said. "Besides, you don't even own a copy—unless it's the Cliff Notes. What's the matter with you? You sound funny."

"Nothing's the matter. What makes you think that?" Two short sentences, but heavy enough to weigh a ton.

"Where's Mattie? She okay?"

"Mattie's fine. The twins and I were giving her a bath. Eddie's in there with them now."

"Then what is it? Something's wrong . . . I can tell."

"Oh, hell, Eliza! I wasn't going to say anything until you got back. Melody called your house again—say, what did you find out?"

"When did she call? What did she say?"

"Just a little while ago—maybe an hour. Your dad answered the phone, told her you weren't going to talk with her unless she came in person."

Eliza's mouth felt dry. "Oh, God! What did she say then?"

"Nothing. Just hung up. Listen, don't worry, Eliza. You know Melody won't do anything to hurt that baby."

"But it's not Melody we're dealing with," Eliza said. "At least, I don't think it is. And it looks like we might have to go to Carrollton to find out for sure."

"Did you have any special plans for tomorrow?" Eliza asked Dorcas over dinner. They had stopped at a steak house on the other side of Charlotte, and Eliza relaxed for the first time that day as she sipped a glass of red wine. She didn't want to drive farther tonight.

Dorcas speared another bite of salad. "What do you have in mind?"

"Minerva's at least another four hours from here, and Syd has Mattie bedded down for the night. There's no reason to rush back home. Why don't we find a place to stay and get an early start in the morning? We could be in Carrollton by noon."

"You don't know how glad I am to hear you say that,"

Dorcas said, smoothing her napkin in place. "Now, I believe I'll try a glass of that wine."

Eliza grinned. "Good, I'll call Dad and tell him we'll see him later tomorrow."

"You realize tomorrow's a Sunday, don't you? Everything will be closed."

"The cemetery will be there, and somebody should be on duty at that mortuary. I want to find out where Marilyn lived—well, actually more about how she died—maybe talk with some of the neighbors."

"And then what?"

"If necessary, I'll try to get the body exhumed. Find out if it really is Marilyn buried there."

The Hemphill brother on duty at the mortuary had gravy on his tie and garlic on his breath. Eliza felt sure they had interrupted his midday meal. "Ah, yes, my brother said you called. That was Mrs. Blodgett now, wasn't it? A young woman—so tragic! Are you a relative?" The undertaker had a morsel of food in his mouth, and he tried to swallow it without being obvious.

Eliza followed him to a small office where he thumbed through a file. "Cousins," she said. "We were out of the country when it happened—such a shock!"

"Yes, of course, I can imagine . . . ah, here it is. Your cousin was interred in Orchard Valley. I can give you directions if you'd like to pay respects."

"We'd like the home address too, if you don't mind. They've moved since we saw them last, and I do want to speak to Arnold . . ." Eliza's voice softened. "Poor Arnold, he must be broken up, bless his heart."

Dorcas nodded. "Yes, bless his heart."

Shaking his head solemnly, the gravy-splotched Hemphill wrote a street address on the other side of a cemetery map. "I don't think you'll have trouble finding the grave site," he said. "It's right at the top of that first hill as you drive in. Her husband said she'd like her ashes buried there, closer to heaven, he said."

"Her ashes?" Eliza almost stumbled on her way out.

"Your cousin was cremated," the mortician explained. "I'm sorry, I thought my brother told you. It was what she would have wanted, her husband said."

"Looks like Arnold cleaned up after himself pretty well," Eliza said as they drove away. "So much for having the body exhumed."

"You really don't want to go by the cemetery, do you?" Dorcas asked. "I don't see much use in it. After all, neither of us knew Marilyn."

"I'd like to stop there just the same," Eliza said softly. "I have a horrible feeling that's not Marilyn in that grave, Dorcas. I'd like to tell Melody good-bye."

Eliza left a pot of pink chrysanthemums, bought hastily at a grocery store, on the new mound of red dirt and made a silent promise to Melody Lamb. It didn't take long.

She was quiet as they drove through peaceful Sunday streets to the address Mr. Hemphill had given them, a shabby-looking area of modest brick bungalows built about forty years before. The yards were small, and for the most part straggly, and the house where the Blodgetts had lived was bordered by a sickly hedge. A "For Rent" sign sat crookedly in the front yard.

Dorcas parked across the street. "Look how high the grass is . . . and the windows are positively naked. Nobody lives there, Eliza."

"But somebody did." Eliza saw two little girls playing in a wading pool in the yard next door while a woman watched from the porch. "Maybe the neighbors know something."

The large woman in the sagging chair squinted as they came up the walk. No, she hadn't known the people next door. She was only minding them babies for a couple of hours, so their mama, her daughter, could get a little rest. "Works the second shift, you know, and her third one's due in October." She attempted to stir up a little air with one of those old cardboard fans with a picture of Jesus on it. "I heard Wanda moving around in there while ago," she said, rising with great effort. "Let me go see if she's dressed."

Eliza started to protest, but the woman opened the door, stuck her head inside, and yelled. She didn't really have to do that. The screen had a hole in it as big as a watermelon.

Except for her bulging stomach, Wanda was as thin as her mother was fat; she looked as if she could do with a blood transfusion, and a good haircut wouldn't hurt either. Yet there was something almost beautiful about her as she watched her children playing there. "You, Wilene!" she yelled at one of the waders. "Go dry off and sit in the sun, you're turning blue." She turned curious eyes to her two visitors, and although Eliza wore casual pants and sandals, she felt overdressed.

"Yeah, I knew them some," Wanda said when Eliza explained why they had come. "That was awful what happened! They say she lay in that tub all day until her husband come home and found her."

"Oh, so he wasn't there when it happened?" Eliza sat on the steps beside her, although she hadn't been invited.

"Oh, no, he was out on a job—somewhere over in Newnan, and didn't get home until late. Came over here crying and carrying on—plumb tore up, and who could blame him?" She clapped her hands twice. "Come on, Trudy, you too—time to get out! You've been in long enough—I mean it."

"What does her husband do? I don't believe she ever said, did she, Dorcas?"

Her neighbor shook her head and looked as if she wished she were somewhere else. A curl of iron gray hair had come loose from her neat bun, and Dorcas concentrated on tucking it in place.

"Works for some kind of home improvement company. You know, they install that siding, do roofing, painting—stuff like that," Wanda told them. "He left early that morning just as I was getting home from my shift, and they say she must've died sometime around noon . . . just lay there in that water all that time."

Eliza tried not to picture that. "Had they been here long?"

"'Bout a year, I guess. I didn't know'em real good, her not having kids and all, but they always spoke or waved when we saw them. I gave them tomatoes last year from my daddy's garden, and they got our mail for us a couple of times when we went out of town." Wanda looked over at the house next door. "Arnold and Elroy—that's my husband—well, sometimes they talked baseball together. That's where Elroy is now; plays for Dunn's Garage." She sighed. "Still can't believe she's gone."

"What about her husband?" Dorcas asked. "Arnold. What happened to him?"

"Said he couldn't stand being in that house without her —memories and all," Wanda told them.

"Do you know where we could find him?"

"No tellin'. Don't think he even works at the same place anymore. Told Elroy he wanted to put this town behind him. Poor thing. Some folks just can't handle grief, you know."

CHAPTER TWENTY-THREE

"Now what?" Dorcas said as they left the forlorn row of bungalows behind them.

"Wanda said Marilyn worked part time as a waitress at some restaurant downtown. Can't remember the name of it. Lord, I should've written it down!" Eliza rubbed her aching forehead. Her eyes burned like they had soap in them.

"*The Golden Goose.* How could you forget that? I think she said it's on the left past the college. Hope they're open, we haven't had anything since breakfast."

"I'm not hungry," Eliza said as they pulled into a parking lot behind the restaurant.

But she was. Eliza meant to order a salad, but the man at the table next to theirs was having the special of the day: baked hen with sweet potatoes, rice and green beans cooked with a piece of side meat. Eliza had the same and the apple cobbler too.

The middle-aged woman who waited on them hadn't known Marilyn well, although the thought of what had happened "made her go clean cold all over." The dark-haired girl at the cash register knew Marilyn better than anybody there, she told them. "Her and Marilyn was right good friends. Took it kinda hard, I think."

The cashier, who wore a pin naming her Tina, was reluctant to talk about Marilyn at first, but she mellowed when Dorcas commented on the diamond engagement ring she wore. She was marrying in September, she said, finally smiling, and Marilyn was to have been a brides-maid. "I've already ordered the dresses too. Now I guess I'll have to ask my cousin . . . she's about that same size."

Since most of the lunchtime customers had left, Tina led them to a table to talk. Marilyn had worked there since right before Christmas, she said, and the two of them found they had a lot of things in common. They liked to shop together, and sometimes went to bars with Arnold and Tina's boyfriend. And once in a while, Tina told them, they'd just order pizza and watch videos at her place.

"Did she ever have you over?" Eliza asked. "I mean for dinner or something?"

Tina shrugged. "Marilyn didn't cook much. I stopped by once to bring groceries when she was out with the flu, but she didn't ask me in. Didn't want me to catch it, I reckon."

"Tina, I don't want to upset you by asking this, but I have to know . . . was there ever any suspicion that Ar-nold had anything to do with her death?" Eliza watched the girl's face across the table.

"Oh, no! God, no. Arnold would never do that! Why, if Marilyn told him to jump in the Tallapoosa River, I reckon he would've done it. Besides, he couldn't have. Arnold was over in Newnan all day."

"Are you sure?" Dorcas asked.

"Well, no, but wouldn't the police follow up on that? I mean the husband's always the first one they think of, isn't he?"

Eliza nodded. She had a point there. "Do you know where he went?"

Tina twisted the ring on her finger. "Haven't heard a word. Just said he had to get away." She looked up. "Reckon he'll come back?"

Eliza didn't think so. "What does Arnold look like? Marilyn told us about him, but we never had a chance to meet."

Tina smiled, and for the first time, Eliza noticed how expressive her eyes were. "Handsome! Tall, dark and handsome. Arnold Blodgett could pass for a movie star, I guess." Tina giggled. "But he's not as cute as my Raymond!"

"What kind of car does he drive?" Eliza hoped Tina wouldn't ask why she wanted to know.

"I don't know. Something blue—a Plymouth I think. He used to drive this big old black thing, but they traded it in last spring. We kidded him about it—looked just like a hearse."

"I wish she'd had a picture of him—even a little snapshot," Eliza said as they drove back to Minerva. "We need something to go on."

"Well, there's the car," Dorcas said. "Tina wasn't sure of the make, but I expect the neighbors would know, and if it's the one you saw, you know the last two digits on the license number."

"If he still has it." Eliza watched Herefords grazing in a daisy-dotted pasture as they rumbled over a bridge. "That was a blue car in front of us when I was rescued from Dogwood Park; kind of a dark blue, I think. Could've been a Plymouth. I asked Tina to call me if she heard from him."

"Do you think she will?"

"I don't think she'll get the chance," Eliza said. "Arnold Blodgett is 'laying low.' He won't come out of hiding until he thinks it's safe."

Dorcas sighed. "Wish you'd gotten a good look at him. But then, if wishes were horses . . ."

"If wishes were horses, what?" Eliza waited, smiling.

"If wishes were horses, it would be kinda crowded in this car," Dorcas said. "Kinda messy too."

Eliza grabbed the arm rest as they rounded a sharp curve. Maybe she shouldn't have eaten all that dessert. "I know somebody who did see Arnold Blodgett," she said. "Dorcas, we've got to find Penny Shillinglaw!"

"Didn't you say she was staying with relatives?"

"That's what her mother told me." Eliza frowned. "I really don't blame her for keeping Penny's whereabouts a secret. If Marilyn thought she knew something, she could be in trouble."

Dorcas thought about that a minute. "Let's hope Penny takes showers," she said.

Eliza groaned. "Didn't you say your nephew knew her uncle?"

"Whose uncle?"

"Penny's. Luke went to school with him, didn't he?"

Dorcas nodded. "High school, yes, but it's been more than a couple of years ago."

"Could you think of an excuse to call him? Maybe invent a class reunion or something."

"Harold McIver? Why would Luke want a reunion with him? Couldn't stand him when they were in school together!" Dorcas blew her horn at a stray chicken.

"Maybe he'll tell you where Penny is if you play it right," Eliza said. "Mention casually that she's a neighbor of ours . . . you've noticed how fast she's growing up . . . garbage like that. Be coy."

Dorcas looked almost scary. "I've never paid much attention to that little girl at all—and I wouldn't know how to be *coy!* However, I'll think of something if you really think it's necessary."

Eliza smiled. "It's necessary. In fact, it's downright essential."

Ben Figg was waiting on the front porch when they got

home. "That policeman called," he told Eliza. "Said to let him know when you got back."

"Kemper? Did he say what he wanted?"

"Didn't give a clue. Eliza, where've you been?"

"I told you, Daddy, we spent the weekend in North Carolina."

"It wouldn't have anything to do with Melody, would it?" he said.

Oh, Lord! Should she tell him? No, not yet. "Hey, speaking of Melody—any more phone calls? Is Mattie okay?"

"Yes and no." Ben Figg led her up the steps with an arm about her shoulders. "Yes, Mattie's fine; and no, Melody or whoever she is—hasn't called back . . . but that other guy did."

"What other guy?"

Her father frowned. "What *was* his name . . . ? Charles! Left his number, said give him a call when you can."

Dorcas kicked off her shoes and flopped on the sofa. "That's the second time, Eliza. Call the man, won't you?"

"As soon as you call Harold," Eliza said.

"Harold? Harold who?" Ben wanted to know.

Dorcas laughed as she reached for the telephone. "Harold-Hums-Under-His-Breath. Now hush, you all, and let me concentrate. I have to do a little spy-work here."

She was trying to locate an old classmate of her nephew's, Dorcas told Harold McIver; her stiff, deadpan expression looked almost painful. And did he happen to have an address for so-and-so? He thought they might have kept in touch . . . *No? What a shame! Well . . . so, how've you been? Don't suppose you get home often? Busy . . . yes, I know, Luke too.* Dorcas rolled her eyes and proceeded to feed him the very line about his niece she'd said she couldn't do. *Penny. Yes, lovely girl. Baby-sits for that cute little Mattie next door.* Dorcas sat up straighter and smiled. She actually was enjoying this.

We've missed seeing her lately, but a popular girl like that . . . Oh, really? How nice! Her neighbor couldn't get off the phone fast enough. *Well, it's been nice talking with you, too, Harold . . . A reunion? Yes, you'll have to do that. I know Luke would just love to come . . .*

Dorcas beamed. "She's with her grandmother in El-lijay. Got a summer job in a cousin's shoe store."

"Has to be her dad's parents, since the McIvers are from around here." Eliza reached for the phone. "Penny's dad is a Junior, I think . . . what is his name . . . ? Willis! That's it." Eliza called information, then dialed the number and waited while the telephone rang repeatedly on the other end. "Nobody there," she said. "Must've gone for a Sunday drive."

"We'll try again tonight," Dorcas said. "Shouldn't you give Kemper a call?"

"Not until I talk with Syd. I want my baby back. I want to see Mattie."

"Eliza." Dorcas took her by the shoulders and gently stroked the hair from her forehead. Eliza was surprised at the gesture because her neighbor wasn't usually demonstrative. "Just remember Mattie isn't *your* baby," she said. "At least not yet."

"I know." Eliza called Sydney's familiar number. Her eyes were burning again. She knew Mattie didn't belong to her. Why did Dorcas have to remind her?

She was jolted when the McClanahan's answering machine clicked into play. "We're home!" Eliza said at the beep. "Give me a call when you get in and I'll come and collect my—I'll come and take Mattie off your hands." Eliza frowned. "That's funny. Wonder where they could be?"

Ben looked at his watch. "Well, it's almost six o'clock. Maybe they went somewhere for dinner. Which reminds me, I'd better get going, or Livvy will wonder where I am!"

"With all those kids?" Eliza shook her head.

"I expect they went to Eddie's mom's," Dorcas said. "You could give her a call there."

Eliza went to the kitchen for a glass of tea. "I'll wait; hate to interrupt their supper. Besides, you're right. I need to talk with Kemper. Maybe he can get the details of Marilyn's death from the Carrollton police. Wonder what he wanted?"

What Kemper Mungo wanted, he told her, was to share a piece of information on Jessie Gilreath's death. "Chief Asbury finally gave me permission to do a little investigating over there," he said. "I had them check for prints —especially in the bathroom area. Found several sets that weren't Jessie's around the tub, and then again on the banister leading to the second floor. A man's, I think. Didn't belong to the maid."

"I think I know who they do belong to," Eliza said, and she told him about tracking down Marilyn Gaines. "A woman identified as Marilyn was *accidentally* electrocuted, then conveniently cremated right after Melody disappeared. Now her husband has vanished. If we can find Arnold Blodgett, I think we'll find Marilyn."

Kemper Mungo cleared his throat. "Marilyn?"

"Melody Lamb—or what's left of her, is buried in that grave in Orchard Cemetery," Eliza told him. "I think Marilyn and her husband snatched Melody while she was walking that morning, then murdered her and passed her off as Marilyn."

There was silence on the other end of the line. "But why on earth would they do that?" Kemper asked.

"For the insurance, why else?" Eliza said.

CHAPTER TWENTY-FOUR

The telephone rang at a little after seven that night just as Eliza was getting ready to call Syd at Eddie's parents.

"Eliza?" Sydney sounded breathless. "Thank goodness you're home! I've tried to call there three times and the line was busy."

"Syd? What's wrong? Where are you?" She didn't like the sound of this.

"We're in Atlanta with Olivia . . . listen, I didn't know what else to do! That woman—the one who calls herself Melody—phoned this afternoon. Said she knew I had Mattie and wanted me to know she'd be watching. Watching and waiting, she said."

Eliza clutched the receiver. "Oh." That's all she could say, just, "Oh." She couldn't bring herself to ask the obvious question.

"I'd just gotten the little ones down for a nap," Syd went on, "so I hated to wake them. Besides, I thought, Let her come! Just let her try something!"

"Where was Eddie?" Eliza asked.

"He and Mac went on some kind of Cub Scout thing to Kennesaw Mountain. Lord, I hope he finds the note I left. Anyway, later when I looked out the window, there she was, parked across the street . . . at least I guess it was her. I didn't recognize the car."

"Was it blue?"

"No, this one was white. Then the next time I looked, it was gone. But it kept circling, coming back—just like a shark."

"Why didn't you call the police?" Eliza asked.

"I did, but Kemper wasn't there, and the pea-brain who answered said they couldn't do anything if she wasn't breaking the law." Sydney whispered something aside to somebody, then continued. "Finally I just gathered up the whole group and took them over to Eddie's folks. Didn't tell them about the white car; his mom would have a fit and fall in it."

"What about Mattie?" There. Finally, it was out.

"She's right here. Mattie's fine. I was afraid to take her to your house," Syd said. "She was probably watching that too, and Dorcas was with you, so I just called Olivia and told her I was coming." Sydney stopped for breath. "And here we are!

"Okay . . . just a minute," Syd said to someone else.

"Listen, I'm getting ready to leave for home." She added, "How 'bout calling Eddie and letting him know I'm on my way?"

"I will, Syd, and thanks. Be careful, will you? Call me when you get home, okay?"

The baby would be fine, Olivia assured her. Although Eliza might not remember, her father had looked after babies before, and the two of them could beg, borrow or buy enough to get by.

"She's already fed and bathed," Olivia told her. "And I'll take a few days off and take care of her myself. I want to do this—really! Try not to worry, Eliza. Mattie will be safe with us. For all that woman knows, Syd left her with Eddie's mother. Nobody knows she's here."

But how could they be sure?

Eliza was relieved when Sydney called later to tell her she reached home safely. "Sorry to shake you up like that," Syd said. "It was all I could think to do at the time."

"You did the right thing," Eliza said. "I'm the one who should be apologizing to you. I put your whole family in danger going away like I did. I shouldn't have left Mattie."

"Don't be silly. You learned something, didn't you?"

"More than I really wanted to know," Eliza admitted. And if she could ever reach Penny Shillinglaw, maybe she could begin to fit the pieces together.

Eliza waited until after Dorcas had come down the next morning to try the Ellijay number again, and was relieved when Penny's grandmother answered.

"She's right here—just finished breakfast," the woman said. Thank goodness she didn't ask who Eliza was or what she wanted. Now, if she could just keep Penny on the line.

But the girl was surprisingly polite, and even seemed glad Eliza had called. "How did you find me?" she asked.

"Oh, I have my spies," Eliza said, with a look at her neighbor. "Penny, we need to talk. It's about what happened to Melody."

"I know. I wanted to tell you before, but Mom . . . well, she thought I'd get in some kind of trouble. I've been so worried. I just feel awful!" Was Penny crying? "I didn't mean anything, honest. I won't have to go to jail, will I?"

"No, of course not! But you might know something that could help us find out what happened. It's not too late, you know."

Eliza waited. Over a hundred miles away in Ellijay she

could hear a soft whimpering sound. She hoped it was a sigh of relief. "There was a man," Penny began.

"Arnold?"

"Who? Well, he called himself Arnie. Cute. Looked a little like Elvis . . . like when he was young and handsome. Before he got fat, you know."

"Where did you meet him?" Eliza couldn't remember seeing anyone like that.

"Well, you know the Phylers that live around the block from us? They're adding to their house. Gonna have a rec room with a big deck out back and everything. And see, I stopped by to look at it one day when I was jogging. That's when I met Arnie. He kinda flirted like, and I guess I flirted back."

So that's why Penny was so dedicated to her daily exercise.

"Nobody could blame you for that," Eliza said. "You didn't do anything wrong. Do you remember what he said?"

"Yeah, he knew I sat with Mattie, and asked me all about Melody. One day I told him about The Boss. How I fed him, and everybody was scared of him but me. Especially Melody. He kept wanting to talk about that. Thought it was funny, I guess."

"Did he want to know about her walks?"

"You know, I didn't think about it until later, but I guess he did in a way. Asked me if many people in the neighborhood walked for exercise, or if I was the only one. I told him Melody took the baby out every morning. And he liked to talk about the Thornbroughs' dog, too. What he liked to eat, what made him act mean—stuff like that. Said he was thinking about getting one—a dog like The Boss. Couldn't imagine why anybody would want a dog like that, I told him."

The ham bone. How could she word this without laying a huge guilt trip on this child? "You said the dog liked ham bones," Eliza said. "Did Arnold—Arnie know that?"

Penny paused for a minute. "Yeah, he knew. That's

why he asked me all those questions. He must've bribed that dog with a ham bone so it would run after Melody. That's how he got her in his car. Because I told him about it . . . and now Melody's gone. But I didn't know . . . I didn't know . . ." Penny Shillinglaw began to cry.

Eliza swallowed hard. She wasn't going to get teary! "Look, Penny, this Arnie could just as easily have found all this out from somebody else. We know you didn't realize . . . just try to put it behind you, promise?"

"I'll try," the girl said timidly.

"How long will you be staying in Ellijay?"

"About another month. Daddy wants me to get work experience, he says, and I'm saving for a car, you know."

"Good. That's good," Eliza said. "And don't mention what you've told me to anybody else."

"Do you think she'll be safe there?" Eliza asked Kemper when they talked later that morning. She had told him about Penny's conversations with Arnold Blodgett, which only confirmed what they already guessed.

Ben had called before breakfast to let them know all was well in Atlanta, so Eliza went in to work at the usual time. She had tried unsuccessfully to reach Kemper earlier by phone, and was relieved to see him pull into the parking lot at Bellawood a little before noon.

"Penny Shillinglaw doesn't come across as the type to be suspicious," Kemper said. "I doubt if Arnold even remembers who she is."

"I hope you're right," Eliza said. But Arnold wasn't the one who worried her. "Syd had to take Mattie to my—uh —to Olivia's in Atlanta yesterday because of Marilyn's threats." She told him about the phone call and the strange white car.

"So I heard," he said. "It might not have been who Syd thought it was, but I wish she'd taken the tag number just the same."

"Why is she doing this? If it is Marilyn—and I'm almost sure it is, why does she keep calling? What could she possibly want with Mattie?"

Kemper Mungo stood in her office window looking over the shady grounds below. "You forget. She wants us to believe she is Melody. For all she knows, that's what we think . . . and Melody would want her baby back." He stroked the old oak window frame as if it helped him to think. "I believe this woman is trying to convince us that Melody is still alive, so we'll accept that Marilyn is the one who died. I really don't think she wants the baby at all."

"Oh, how I'd like to believe that! Did you find out anything about the way she died? Are they absolutely certain the husband had nothing to do with it?"

"Well, he wasn't there; they're sure of that. His alibi checks out. Arnold Blodgett never left his job over in Newnan."

"Weren't the police over there suspicious about it at all?" Eliza asked.

Kemper sat on the windowsill and stretched his long legs in front of him. "Police are always suspicious about an accidental death, but they said a bracket was loose that held the shelf above the bathtub. Looked like it just tilted and the radio slid into the water. They thought she might've reached for something and grabbed it by accident, like you do when you have soap in your eyes. Looked like she'd been washing her hair, they said."

"But we know better." Eliza looked past him at a squirrel scampering along an oak limb and wished she could feel as free and unburdened. How long would this go on?

"Did you tell them what we suspect?" she asked.

"Yes, and they're looking into it. The thing is . . . they don't know where Arnold is either." Kemper straightened a picture on the wall, flipped through the pages of a catalog, and tossed it aside. "The officer I spoke with called back to tell me they'd gotten in touch with the insurance company that held the policy on Marilyn Blodgett's life."

"And . . . ? For heaven's sake, light somewhere, will you, Kemper? You're making me nervous."

He plopped into a convenient chair. "And they're processing the claim. In fact, a check should've gone out this week, but they're sitting on it until we clear this up."

"How much?"

Kemper shrugged. "A lot. He didn't tell me the amount, just said it was enough so the Blodgetts wouldn't have to worry about money for a long time. Marilyn took it out on herself a little over a year ago. Her husband, of course, is the beneficiary."

"So, if nobody knows where they are, how will they know where to send it?" Eliza asked.

"He left a forwarding address. A post office box number."

"What post office? Where?"

"Right outside Atlanta. That little branch near Dogwood Park." Kemper Mungo shook his head as he started for the door. "That's all they're waiting for, those two. When—and if that check comes in, they'll be outa here!"

The sky was skimmed with clouds by the time Eliza got home that evening, and the temperature had dropped about ten degrees. It looked as if it might rain, but not anytime soon. Eliza glanced at the teapot clock over the stove. If she hurried, she would have time for a walk. She not only needed the exercise, but the time to think as well.

Since Mattie was in Atlanta, Eliza had sent her neighbor home. Dorcas had kept books for her husband's construction company until his death several years before, and seemed to be even busier than when she worked on a regular basis. "There's no need in your staying here," Eliza told her. "I'm sopping up your valuable time, and I know you have better things to do. Go on! Get outa here, and do something—go somewhere . . . have fun."

"My goodness, you're getting to be a regular little dictator," Dorcas said. "And what if I don't want to go?"

"All right. Look me in the eyes and tell me you don't want to go."

Dorcas Youngblood straightened her well-padded

shoulders and squared off. "Eliza," she said. "I don't want to go . . . without your knowing where to find me. But I have been promising my nephew I'd come to see their new home in Milledgeville." She scribbled a number on a piece of paper. "I'll only be gone a few days—now, call me if you need me. Promise?"

Now Eliza pulled on comfortable shorts and scrambled in her closet for walking shoes. She would take her radio along, listen to that good jazz station. Maybe it would take her mind off her problems for a little while. Eliza sat on the bed to tie her shoes. Now where did she put that radio?

Radio. That man in the park had returned it. Olivia said he had telephoned too, and she hadn't even bothered to thank him. If it hadn't been for Charles, she might be in a little urn alongside of whoever was buried in Orchard Valley.

Eliza found his number taped to the refrigerator and dialed. If he was out, she would just leave a message and tell him, "Thank-you-very-much!" And that would be the end of that.

But someone picked up the phone on the third ring. "Charlie English."

Good. Eliza had forgotten his last name. She thanked him for bringing the radio and apologized for being late in returning his call. "My neighbor and I were doing a little research this weekend: trying to track down the Phantom of the Park!"

He chuckled. "And did you?"

"In a way." Eliza told him what they had learned about Melody's twin. "We think Marilyn and her husband are somewhere in the area," she said. "I just hope the police can find them before they get suspicious and vamoose."

"That's one reason I called," Charlie English said. "Remember that car we saw in the park that day? The one you thought that guy was driving? Well, I saw one like it last week—recognized it from the dent on the rear fender, and the license plate ended in 48. I'm pretty sure the same man was driving . . . anyway, I followed him, did a little checking."

"Where did he go? Do you know where he lives?"

"Went into a gym over on Lumpkin Avenue. I gave up on him before he came out, but the guy who works at the front desk said he comes about three times a week, usually on the same days."

"Was anyone with him?" Eliza asked.

"Not when I saw him," Charlie said. "But he was back there again on Thursday—in a white car this time. The guy at the desk says he pays in cash. Name's Arnie."

CHAPTER TWENTY-FIVE

"The police are looking for that man," Eliza said. "Do you know where he lives?"

"I got a quick look at the sign-in book the last time I saw him there. Just gives a box number."

Eliza groaned. "This could take forever! Kemper—that's one of our local police—said he'd talk to somebody on the force there and see if they could stake out that post office; it's the branch out near the park. He didn't sound too encouraging though; first of all, they're not convinced the guy has really *done* anything. Besides, they don't have the manpower to watch the place all the time. And who knows when this Arnie comes in for his mail? He might wait until the middle of the night. But if he's a regular at this gym, maybe our chances are looking up."

"The two of them must have had this plan in the works for a good while," Charlie said. "You said she took out that policy over a year ago." He hesitated. "I hope you're being careful, Eliza. She sounds determined . . . and more than a little crazy."

"I know. I probably shouldn't even be talking to you about it. I've already wasted most of my neighbor's summer, and put my best friend's family in danger. If you're smart, you won't get involved. I feel like Typhoid Mary."

"Which brings me to the other reason for calling," Charlie said.

"What? Typhoid Mary?"

"No, getting involved. I called to invite you to dinner."

"Oh. When?"

"How long does it take to drive to Minerva? I could be there by eight."

Eliza glanced at herself in the mirror. Stringy hair, no makeup. It would take about that long to get presentable. "What happened to Green Eyes and Limping Foot?"

"Who?"

"The girl you were with in the park. I sort of got the idea you two were a couple."

He laughed. "Oh, you mean Andrea! Well, unfortunately, she thought so too.

"I realize that's a long time to wait for dinner," he said. "But I know a little Italian place just a few miles from there that will make it worth your while."

"I promise I'll be hungry," Eliza said, resisting the temptation to snatch a couple of oatmeal cookies Dorcas had left earlier. She decided to walk instead. There should be just enough time to circle a few blocks, then shower and change before Charlie English was due.

Charlie English. Eliza tried to remember his face. It was a nice face, but not remarkable. Light brown hair . . . and his eyes . . . she couldn't remember the color of his eyes, but he laughed easily. She had felt comfortable with Charlie English. And when was the last time she had heard from the audacious Spencer G. Fillmore? Not even a consoling phone call when her mother died! Eliza walked faster. It felt good to be looking forward to going out to dinner with a compatible male. It had been a long time since she had been genuinely enthusiastic about a date.

Eliza hurried past the intersection of Habersham and Henry Grady where Melody had vanished a month before. Would she ever go down this street without remembering that awful morning? She waved at Diane Fossett out watering her flowers. The Fossett boy had probably been the last person, other than her kidnappers, to see Melody Lamb alive. Now Eliza would think of that when she looked at their trim ranch house.

Martha Figg had always referred to the Fossett place as "new," even though it was built about thirty years before. Habersham Street was in the older part of town, and when her great grandfather had built there, it was the main residential street in Minerva. A few blocks away, Eliza passed the old Trull house where Miss Mamie and Miss Inez, sisters in their eighties, lived without speaking to one another. One had married the other's boyfriend, the story went, then returned as a widow to claim her half of the family home.

Across the street Lillian Mahaffey, Minerva's head librarian, waved to Eliza as she locked the massive front door of the log cabin building that housed the town's collection of books. Begun in the early part of the century, the library was been added to through the years, but it still maintained the charm of it's original plan. Wisteria climbed over the huge stone chimney and twisted past Queen Anne windows to cascade over the rustic porch. Eliza had spent happy hours reading there, and it relaxed her just to look at it. Whoever kidnapped Melody had passed along these very streets. Had Melody known she was going to die?

By the time Charlie arrived, Eliza had let hot water pound her until she felt she might dissolve down the drain. With her clean hair coaxed into turning under at the right places, and wearing a flower-splashed print she knew became her, Eliza found herself tentatively slipping into the old Eliza. The carefree Eliza who had left this house to go to college, and then on to the Peace Corps and grad school, planning never to come home to stay.

But here she was. Now something awful had happened to Melody, and she had to find out why. Eliza Figg had made it this far, and she had a sneaking premonition she was going to like herself if she lived through it.

Maybe it was the walk.

Charlie English showed up at the door in a nubby green sports coat and a tie with dinosaurs on it. "My sister gave it to me as a joke," he explained. "When I was a kid, I used to live and breathe dinosaurs." Oddly, it went well with the rest of his attire.

In coat and tie, Charlie English bore little resemblance to the rain-soaked walker Eliza had latched onto in Dogwood Park, but his sense of humor remained the same. He was managing editor, and sometimes reporter for a small suburban newspaper outside Atlanta, she learned, and his tales of the things that went on there made her laugh: The handwritten wedding writeup giving an account of a couple in clown costumes who married at the skating rink to the background of an Elvis medley. (Did they spend their honeymoon at 'Heartbreak Hotel?' Eliza asked.) Or the stubby little man in Hawaiian shirt and Bermuda shorts who wanted to put an ad in the paper seeking information on the S.O.B. who ran off with his wife.

They shared an aversion to ill-used words and phrases, Eliza found, and listed them as they sat over after-dinner coffee: *most unique* (can't be compared), *end result* (redundant), *at this point in time*—(Eliza admitted she just wanted to slap people who said that. Charlie was in favor of hanging.)

For an hour or so, Eliza Figg shoved the events of the last few weeks behind her, but there was no avoiding the subject when they drove back to Minerva to find Kemper Mungo waiting on her porch.

"What's wrong?" Eliza raced across the lawn. "Has anything happened to Mattie?"

He came down the steps to meet her. "It's okay . . .

didn't mean to scare you. Your friend Sydney got another call tonight, and we didn't know where you were. Just wanted to be sure everything's okay."

"I'm fine; we just went out to dinner." Eliza was dismayed to find her hands were shaking as she introduced the two men. "What did that crazy woman want this time?"

Kemper frowned. "Same thing. Wanted to know where Mattie was."

"Good. Then she must think the baby's still in Minerva." Eliza started for the door. "Come inside for coffee?"

"Not for me, thanks. It's been a long day. Just stopped to see if you were all right." Kemper hesitated at the steps. "Call if there's a problem?"

"I will—and what about surveillance at the post office, Kemper? Are the police there going to cooperate?"

"Sort of half-heartedly, I'm afraid. They said they'd keep an eye out."

"*Keep an eye out!* What good will that do? That means next to nothing! They'll never catch them at this rate," Eliza said. "Besides, Charlie says Arnold's a regular at the Lumpkin Avenue Gym. They might have a better chance of finding him there."

"Oh? Since when?" Kemper looked as if Eliza had told him she'd just taken a vow of silence.

"Since last week." Charles English explained how he had happened to follow Arnold Blodgett to his afternoon workout.

"Charlie's the one who saved me from a muddy fate in Dogwood Park," Eliza said.

Charlie raised an eyebrow. "Did I have a choice? You practically threw yourself at me."

"Joke if you must," Eliza said. "But there's a wild woman running around out there passing herself off as Melody, and I think we all know Mattie won't ever see her mother again."

Kemper squeezed his hat as if he meant to wring it out,

and emitted a soft, dark sigh. "I wasn't going to tell you this, but I checked with the North Carolina Department of Records today. Somebody using Melody's name requested a copy of her birth certificate last month." He looked at Eliza with solemn brown eyes. "Needed it for a passport, I expect."

Eliza heard herself gasp. "Oh, God! What do we do now?"

"*We?* What do you mean we? Just let us take care of this, Eliza. I mean it! Chief Asbury is looking into this thing with the insurance company. Be patient. Sometimes these things just take a little time." Kemper Mungo jammed his hat on his head so hard Eliza expected to hear it rip.

"We don't have a little time," Eliza said to his back.

"What?" He stopped in mid-stride.

"Nothing. You tell Chief Asbury I won't be holding my breath."

"I wonder what would happen if I wrote Arnold Blodgett a letter," Eliza said as they took their coffee into the sitting room. "The post office in Carrollton would forward it to that box number, and Marilyn would know her game was over."

"Then you'd never find them." Charlie bit into one of Dorcas's cookies.

"I guess not. What I'd like to do is get them to lead me to Marilyn, but I'm not up to dealing with Arnold—especially if he's been pumping iron." Eliza leaned back in her chair. It had rained while they were in the restaurant, but a cooling breeze still lingered and the house smelled of the red climbing rose that trailed past the window. "What days did you say he goes for his workouts?"

Charlie set down his cup gently. "Mondays, Wednesdays and Thursdays. Probably has some kind of job that keeps him away the other days. They have to eat, you know."

"What time? Afternoons? Mornings? Does it vary?"

"Afternoons. Gets there at three, or thereabouts. Probably stays a couple of hours." Charlie frowned. "Why? Didn't you hear what the man said, Eliza? The woman you're dealing with isn't normal. Think what she did to her own sister!"

"I know. Frankly, I'm scared to death of her. But she couldn't do anything in public, and I wouldn't let her come here while I'm alone."

"Oh? And what's to keep her from it?"

Eliza punched into a sofa pillow. "If she calls here again, I'll agree to meet her with Mattie—only I won't really bring the baby, of course, but she won't know that. Not until it's too late." Eliza smiled. "I'll arrange it at a time when her hubby's at the gym. Three's a crowd, you know."

"And four's a quartet, but if you insist on doing this, I want to be there." Charles English stood to go. "Back off on this thing, Eliza. You're acting like your elevator doesn't go all the way to the top. Why are you doing this? Is it worth it?"

"I'm doing it for Melody," Eliza said. "And Mattie. And I'm doing it for me. Besides, I don't like people who tamper with other people's lives."

He stood in the doorway. "You will call, won't you, as soon as you hear? I want to be there when the lid blows."

"Think what a story it will make," Eliza said.

Later, unable to sleep, Eliza listened to the faint whirring of the ceiling fan in her bedroom and tried to fit the pieces together.

Why had Melody Lamb not known about her twin? If the information was on Marilyn's birth certificate, wouldn't it be on her sister's as well?

The rotation of the fan blades made vague swirling shadows in the limpid glow of the street light, and Eliza was beginning to feel slightly dizzy from watching it.

Oh, to hell with it! Restlessly she threw aside the sheet to pad zombielike into Melody's room and fumble in the closet for the small metal box she had brought from storage. It had to be here! Surely Melody kept a copy of her own birth certificate. Didn't everyone? Eliza remembered looking through the box earlier. How could she have missed it?

But she had. Melody Gaines's Certificate of Birth was tucked inside an envelope with a poem she had written in the third grade and her diploma from Laurens W. Hill-house Elementary School. A suspicious black ink blot obliterated the line denoting *other live births.*

Eliza shoved it back inside the envelope feeling slightly sick. Lynda Gaines hadn't wanted her daughter to know she had a twin!

CHAPTER TWENTY-SIX

Across the street Jessie Gilreath's house loomed dark and silent. Earlier Eliza had noticed the bright geraniums still sprouting above the window box.

Jessie would never have opened her door to Arnold Blodgett, Eliza thought as she crawled back into bed. But she would've let Melody come inside. Begrudgingly, perhaps, but after all, Jessie had known her as a child.

If Melody Lamb had come to her back door on the pretext of borrowing, say a few eggs or a cup of sugar, Jessie would have complied. (Hoping, no doubt, to share in the resulting baked goods.)

Only it wasn't Melody, but her twin, who stood on the threshold.

But what about Arnold and the dog? Eliza doubted if he would trust a bloodthirsty animal just deprived of a ham bone in the backseat of his car. No, The Boss would be shoved unceremoniously into the trunk to work up an appetite for *ankles tartare,* while Arnold drove into the gravel turnaround behind Jessie Gilreath's house. There

he would be out of sight to neighbors and passersby . . .
until Marilyn called him inside.

Eliza flopped onto her stomach and yawned. Think of
something positive, something cheerful, she told herself
as she closed her aching eyes. She wondered where
Spencer G. Fillmore was and what he was doing. Eliza
tried to remember what he had looked like the last time
they were together, but instead she saw Charlie English's
face.

The phone rang just as Eliza was in the middle of a
most pleasant dream involving a sailboat, vivid turquoise
water, and someone's hand warm on her back. She
bolted awake wide eyed and grabbed the receiver from
the nightstand. Mattie! Something had happened to Mattie! Her feeble "hello" came out in a choked whisper.

"I have the key to your house," a muted voice said.

"What?" Eliza propped herself on an elbow. "Who is
this?" Marilyn, of course. She knew very well who it was.
But did Marilyn have a key to the house?

"Stay out of things that don't concern you, or I'll use
this key. Don't think I won't—maybe tonight . . . And
this time I'll be coming for *you.*"

"Hey, wait a minute!" Eliza rolled out of bed and
edged nearer the window. The street was dark and
empty. And the caller had hung up.

The first thing she did was check the outside doors.
There were three of them. Ben Figg had installed dead
bolt locks on the front and back doors during a rash of
burglaries several years ago, but he had never gotten
around to changing the lock on the side door that opened
off the room at the back of the house. A spacious, sunny
area next to the kitchen, it had once been Eliza and Katherine's nursery, and later served as a sewing room and
office. Now Eliza used it as sort of a catchall corner for
the books and papers she meant to sort and put away.

Eliza made her way quietly through the dark house.
She was afraid to turn on the lights and glad she didn't

need them. She knew every inch of this old place by touch alone.

If Marilyn had a key, the dead bolt locks wouldn't provide any more security than a daisy chain, but her father had installed sliding bolts, front and back for added protection, and Eliza was relieved to see them in place.

She stumbled over a carton of files and papers in the darkness of the cluttered back room, and tried not to swear as she made her way to the door. It would be easy for someone to break the glass on the door and reach through to open the simple twist-type lock.

Eliza extended a hand to reassure herself the lock— however flimsy—was in place, then slapped her palm to her mouth to keep from yelling. The bolt wasn't fastened!

Eliza leaned against the wall and ran one hand over the door to snap the lock into place. Just outside she could hear insects chirping in the grass, and somewhere close by a cat yowled its lusty serenade. Was anyone else out there? How long had the door been unlocked? She couldn't remember the last time she had checked it. And unlike the front and back doors, this one had no safeguarding chain. It was as if her father had presumed a burglar wouldn't notice or care about the third entrance there.

As a precaution, Eliza shoved a desk in front of it, then piled it high with books. She was on her way upstairs before the thought occurred to her that Marilyn Blodgett might be *inside.*

She cowered. There was no other word for it. Eliza Figg inspected her closet, checked under her bed, locked the door of her room and huddled with her pillow in the dark.

Was that a footstep on the back porch? She sat straighter and listened. Something creaked in the hall outside her door. There . . . again! Eliza jumped when a bug flew into her window screen. Night noises. Ordinary old house noises. Weren't they?

Kemper. She would call Kemper Mungo and ask him to check the house. He would growl and lecture her and say, "I told you so," but at least she would be safe. But Kemper was off duty, and Oscar Watts—well, Marilyn could be swinging from the chandelier waving a machete by the time Oscar got here—and then he probably wouldn't notice her. Of course there was Chief Milton Asbury.

Her eyelids felt as if they were made of cast iron, but she knew she wouldn't sleep again tonight. Not here. Eliza picked up the phone and dialed. "Dorcas? Thank goodness you're home! Thought I saw you come in earlier. Listen, I'm sorry to wake you at this hour, but is your extra bedroom available?"

Tomorrow she would change the locks.

Even with new locks, for the next few days Eliza Figg jumped every time the phone rang, especially at night. Ben and Olivia called daily to give a Mattie report; Syd phoned often using vague excuses in an attempt to check up on her; and although her neighbor denied it, Eliza knew Dorcas Youngblood kept vigil at the kitchen window. If they suspected what she was planning, Eliza knew they would converge and descend upon her with dire predictions and worse. But nothing happened.

"If she calls again, for God's sake, don't let her know you suspect who she is," Kemper told her. "It could blow the whole thing. You're playing with nitroglycerin here, Eliza. The woman's unstable. Just pretend you think she's Melody. Try to be calm, *and then call me.*"

By Thursday Eliza had begun to let down her defenses . . . just a little. Maybe the insurance company had decided to mail the check, and Arnold and Marilyn were on their way to Bora Bora—or wherever escaped criminals went. Or, perhaps both had been nabbed during a daring post office raid which Charlie would cover in his newspaper, and nobody bothered to tell her. Kemper Mungo was suspiciously silent.

And then the telephone rang at Bellawood. It was midafternoon, and Eliza was expecting a call from a museum in Macon that wanted her to conduct a workshop in natural dyes. Eliza reached for her desk calendar to confirm the date.

"I know who has my baby," the voice on the telephone said. "Did you think I wouldn't find her in Atlanta? You can tell them I'm on my way. And this time I mean to have her."

Chapter Twenty-seven

"No! Please, wait a minute!" *Calm down, Eliza, remember what Kemper said: Don't beg. She wants you to beg.* "Melody? I've been waiting for you to call. Why did you leave us that way?" *Keep your voice steady, now. You've got to convince her!* "I'd like to see you," Eliza said. "Just tell me where we can meet. What about that little park by the library? Or the mall . . . in front of the pet shop. I'll bring Mattie . . . she loves to look at the puppies, you know . . ." She was rambling. Desperate. Would Marilyn believe her?

The silence was so taut she could've hung clothes off of it. "How do I know I can trust you?" Marilyn said at last.

That did it! "Have I ever given you reason not to? You trusted me enough to leave me with your baby! I wasn't the one who went off without a word. Melody, you scared us to death! We've been worried about you." Her reasoning told her she wasn't speaking to Melody Lamb, but her mouth just went on spouting. *Watch it, Eliza! You've gone too far.*

"Hey, wait a minute! Okay, okay! All I want is the baby. Tell your parents to have her there in an hour. There's a diner about five miles south of there, just past that big carpet mill—the Blue Carnation, or something like that. Just be there!"

"But they can't get here that soon! It takes more than an hour to drive from Atlanta." *She knows that, Eliza. She's playing with you. Stall! Stall for time.* Eliza looked at her watch. It was five after three. If Charlie's deductions were right, Arnold Blodgett would be in the gym for the next two hours: one less threat to worry about. But she needed time. Time for Olivia to drive from Atlanta; time to try to find a safe place for Mattie. The police would have to deal with Arnold.

"Look, I can't get away from here until after five," Eliza said. "And then there are the baby's things to be packed. Let's say seven." *Almost four hours from now. Good.* "We'll meet you at the diner at seven." Take it or leave it, Eliza thought. Of course she had no intention of going through with her offer.

Marilyn took it. "All right, seven. But you'd better be there on time!"

In the next instant Eliza called Atlanta. Was her step-mother never going to pick up the phone? The telephone rang five times before Olivia answered breathlessly.

"Thank goodness! Where *were* you?"

"Eliza? Mattie and I were out on the patio. What is it? Is something wrong?"

Eliza told her about Marilyn's call. "I don't know where she was calling from," she said. "She may already be in Atlanta, but you need to get Mattie away from there. Now."

"It won't take long to get her things together. Where do you want me to bring her?"

"Here. Bring her here to Bellawood," Eliza said. "I've bought us a couple of hours. By the time you get here, I'll think of what to do. Dad at the frame shop?"

"He was," Olivia said. "But he left early to play golf. I can try to catch him."

"No, it would take too long. Just come," Eliza said. "And hurry!"

Downstairs Genevieve Ellison was training a new class of docents. Eliza heard them stirring below, heard someone laugh. It was a reassuring sound. From her window she watched a family walking back from the old chapel. Baxter Phillips had completed his work on the Pitts family chapel in April, and they had already had two small weddings there. Eliza was glad to be surrounded by people. She hoped they would stick around.

Kemper Mungo was not in when she called the Minerva Police Department. Reluctantly Eliza asked for Chief Asbury who told her Kemper was on a case in Atlanta.

"Is it about Melody Lamb?" Eliza asked. "Look, I need to know. Are they going to arrest Arnold Blodgett?" She told him about Marilyn's call. "I think I've delayed her," Eliza said. "But the woman's so volatile I don't know what she'll decide to do."

"Now you know we can't talk about a case," the chief said. "But I will tell you this: You can forget about this Blodgett guy. We've got him dead to rights." Eliza could just imagine his smug expression. "Now, don't you worry, little lady. By tonight those folks over there should have this thing wrapped up—with a lot of help from the Minerva P.D.!"

Which meant they were taking Charlie's bit of detective work seriously and were lying in wait for Arnie at the gym. Then why hadn't Charlie called?

Eliza phoned the newspaper where he worked.

"Charlie's out on a story," a woman in the newsroom told her. "I don't expect he'll be back for a couple of hours."

Eliza gave her the Bellawood number. "Just ask him to call Eliza," she said. "Tell him it's urgent."

She didn't want to frighten Syd, but it wouldn't be a

bad idea to warn her. After all, Marilyn knew where she lived. She might expect them to take Mattie there. But no one answered the phone at the McClanahans'. Probably at the pool or at a little league game, Eliza thought. And she hated to alarm Dorcas, but somehow she had to find a place to hide Mattie, and Eliza knew she could count on her neighbor to help. Reluctantly, she dialed the familiar number.

All she could do now was wait.

What was keeping Olivia? Eliza paced the upper hall again. Didn't she realize the need to hurry? It was almost five-thirty. If she had left the house two hours ago, she should have been here already. Eliza stood at the window that looked out over the long drive, but there was no sign of Olivia's sleek gray car. What if Marilyn had found them? What if they'd had an accident?

Enough of this! Eliza told herself. You're going to need your head on straight when she gets here. But they had to start soon if they were going to drive to Dorcas's nephew's home in Milledgeville. Dorcas had called to explain that they needed a place of refuge for a few hours —possibly even a night, and Luke and his wife were expecting them.

"Are you sure you don't want me to come out there and wait with you?" her neighbor had asked. But Eliza needed her more at home. "You can keep an eye on things there," she said. "But keep your doors locked! Who knows where Marilyn might show up next."

Now she wished she had accepted Dorcas's offer. Eliza had watched the last visitor drive away twenty minutes ago, and Genevieve Ellison soon followed.

"You sure you'll be all right?" she had called from the downstairs hallway.

"I'm fine. Olivia's going to meet me here in a few minutes," Eliza assured her. "Besides, I have some work to catch up on." It wouldn't do to let Genevieve know what she planned. She wouldn't tell anyone intentionally, but

Genevieve liked to talk, and Marilyn had a knack for finding things out. Eliza wondered where she was now.

She sat at her desk to read over some letters she had written earlier, then signed them and slipped them into envelopes to be ready for tomorrow's mail. Eliza had just sealed the last one when she heard a car in the drive.

Shoving the stack of letters aside, she hurried downstairs. It was about time! What had taken Olivia so long? Eliza hurried outside and looked around for her stepmother. But where was her car? It wasn't in the parking lot. "Olivia?"

"Surprise! I just couldn't wait to see you!" At first she thought Melody Lamb stood under the large magnolia out front, but it wasn't Melody waiting there in a tank top and cut-off jeans. It was her sister Marilyn. Her features were the same, only her hair was parted on the left, and she wore it a little shorter. But it was her eyes that gave her away. They were the same color as Melody's eyes, but they were like looking into a frozen pond. How can two people look so much alike physically, and yet be so different?

And that was when Eliza knew without a doubt that Melody Lamb was dead.

She drew in her breath. "Melody! I didn't expect you. I was just getting ready to leave." Eliza held out a hand. Would the girl expect a hug after all this time? A handshake? Oh God, she didn't want to touch her! Eliza was relieved when she backed away.

"Why don't you follow me? Olivia will meet us at the diner." *Get her away from here! Now, before it's too late.* She felt queasy, weak, as if she had live tadpoles swimming around in her stomach.

"Don't give me that crap," the woman said. "Do you think I'm a fool? I knew you wouldn't bring me that baby." Marilyn Blodgett smiled. "So if it's all the same to you, I'll just wait here for her." And for the first time, Eliza noticed the gun. It was a small black gun; Marilyn held it carelessly at her side as if she weren't aware of it. The sun gleamed blue off the barrel.

Eliza put her hand on the back of a rocking chair. She wanted to sit down, but she was afraid Marilyn might shoot her if she moved. "Why are you doing this?"

Marilyn stepped up on the porch and leaned against the railing, just as if she were a friendly neighbor dropping in for a visit. With one hand she put a cigarette in her mouth and flicked open a lighter. "You can quit pretending now," she said, breathing out a cloud of smoke. "Arnie knows you've been checking up on us. People talk, you know."

Eliza avoided her eyes. "Where's Melody?"

"Where do you think?" She was actually smiling!

"But she was your sister! How could you do that to your own twin?"

Marilyn took another puff and examined the smoke as if she could read something there. "It's not as if we were close," she said. "She didn't even remember me. Besides, it was the only way I could get the money. I had to be dead, you know for Arnie to collect on that policy . . . and now you've made them suspicious! If you've fouled up that check, you can kiss that kid good-bye, you prying little bitch!"

Eliza felt fear spread all the way to her fingertips, down to her toes. This woman wouldn't hesitate to kill her, or anybody else who happened to get in her way. She stood there hoping Olivia had had a flat tire, taken a wrong turn.

If only she had a weapon—anything! Eliza had read about women defending themselves with the spike heels of their shoes, and for the first time regretted wearing comfortable flats. So much for that!

"We should've gotten that check by now," Marilyn said. "Arnie knows they've been watching the post office." She laughed. "You think he doesn't know that? He's been paying some bum to go in and get the mail for him. Had to give him ten bucks." Marilyn stationed herself so she could see a car approaching and squinted into the sun. "If they were smart, they'd watch from the inside, see which box he goes to, but they've got some asshole out front in a car—parked across the street . . . like we wouldn't notice that!"

Eliza wondered if Arnold knew he was being watched at the gym. "But what do you want with Mattie? She's just a baby! What use is she to you?"

"Plenty! But you'll find out if you've blown this for Arnie and me. That insurance money is our ticket outa here. If we don't get it, we'll have to find some other way."

Eliza didn't like the way she said that. "What other way?"

"How much would you and your family be willing to pay to get little Mattie back in one piece?"

"But you don't have her! You haven't already . . ." Eliza thought about throwing the chair at her, but if Marilyn shot her, then what would become of Olivia and Mattie? She had promised Melody she would take care of her baby. She had to stay alive.

"Hell, I'm tired of all this waiting! By the time I caught up with my sister, she was at least five months pregnant. Well, *that* would never do! Then of course we had to get her nerdy husband out of the way! Lucky for us there was nobody around when he went fishing that day. Boating can be so dangerous, don't you think?" Marilyn ground out her cigarette on the newly painted porch floor. "Well, well, looka there. Here she comes now."

Eliza saw a puff of dust at a bend in the driveway and heard the drone of a car approaching. A gray car. Olivia's.

"Just stay right there," Marilyn said, moving back into the shadows of the porch. "We'll let her find us."

Eliza stood like a cigar store Indian with her back against the wall and watched Olivia's car turn into the parking lot. She remembered snatches of things Melody had said: *I meet myself around every corner. . . I'm afraid I'm going to hurt myself. . . . Do you think I'm going crazy if I see people who shouldn't be there?* This explained her almost violent reaction when Dorcas joked about Melody having twins, her dreams of being smothered. She knew something awful was going to happen. Somehow she had known all along.

Olivia brought the car full circle and gave two short blasts on the horn as she parked in the shade of a tree. Behind her in the backseat, Eliza could see the carrier holding Mattie.

CHAPTER TWENTY-EIGHT

arilyn waved the gun just enough for Eliza to read her silent message. She wanted her to stand on the steps so that Olivia would see her, and she wanted her there *now*.

Reluctantly Eliza stepped into the sunlight. Maybe Olivia would see the pleading in her eyes.

But Olivia had already started across the lawn. Why was she leaving the baby in the hot car? Eliza strained to see through the glare of the window. Mattie seemed unusually still and quiet. Was she sick? Or merely asleep?

"Sorry I'm late!" Olivia looked up as she neared the porch and shaded her eyes with her hand. "Took a little detour. Hope you're not going to mind, but—"

"That's far enough." Marilyn stepped forward. "I'll have to ask you to drive just a little farther. I understand there are outbuildings around back?" The last sentence was directed at Eliza.

"I don't believe you've met Marilyn?" Eliza stepped down to take Olivia's hand. Her eyes said, "I'm sorry."

"In the car now—hurry!" Eliza felt Marilyn move up behind her, felt the hard gun in her back.

"What do you want with us? Whose car?" Olivia asked.

"Yours, stupid. I have to get it out of the way. Get in and drive."

Olivia looked at her stepdaughter with desperation in her eyes. "Please don't wake the baby," she said. "She's been running a fever—she's sick."

"If you care so much about the God-damned baby, do as I say, and hurry up about it!" Marilyn got in the front beside Olivia and instructed her to drive. Eliza slid in the back next to the silent infant. What was the matter with Mattie? Olivia hadn't mentioned her being sick earlier.

Marilyn held the gun on Olivia as she drove. "If either of you tries anything, I'll shoot you first, and then the baby. Now, drive around back. I don't want anybody to see this car." She glanced at Eliza. "Yours I'll take care of later.

"What's that building back there through the trees?" Marilyn gestured toward the oak grove.

"Just an old chapel." Eliza reached out to lift the light blanket from Mattie's face. She must be burning up wrapped like that. And Olivia had dressed her too warmly. The baby didn't stir as Eliza touched her hand; she drew back as if she had been burned.

She saw Olivia's frantic eyes in the rearview mirror. "The doctor says to keep her covered," Olivia said. "She's been having chills."

"Thought you said she had a fever." Marilyn glanced at the silent bundle behind her. "What's wrong with her, anyway?"

"Chills. Chills and fever. She has a bad throat—strep infection. Doctor gave her a dose of penicillin," Olivia said. "She'll sleep quietly now." It sounded like a promise.

"This is far enough, oughta do just fine. Pull up out

back here. Now . . . out, both of you!" Marilyn had her hand on the door as they bumped to a stop.

"What do you want us to do?" Eliza asked. "And what about Mattie? I hate to disturb her."

"Then don't! The kid's fine where she is. Let her sleep." Marilyn motioned toward the chapel. "Is this door unlocked?"

Eliza nodded. There was nothing inside to steal.

"Good. Get in here . . . don't stop! Keep walking."

Eliza and Olivia marched silently down the aisle like a reluctant bridal pair. Behind them, Marilyn kept a close pace. Was she going to shoot them here—in the church— at the altar? Eliza felt like the sacrificial lamb. Only Melody had been the Lamb who was sacrificed.

"What's back there?" Marilyn peered behind the simple altar.

"Couple of rooms. Choir room, I guess, and a kind of study. I've only been in here a few times since they did all that work." Eliza felt strangely light-headed, almost euphoric, and she purposely kept her face averted. She knew now if she lived through this day, she would stay right here in Minerva. There were worse places to raise Melody's child—and hers.

Marilyn circled the pulpit, then kicked at a low door in the side of the platform behind it. "See what's in here."

Eliza stepped forward. She knew what was behind the door. It was a cupboard, a small empty cupboard that once held communion vessels, vases and such.

Stick your head in the oven, Gretel, and see if it's hot enough. Now Marilyn was going to shoot them both and leave them in a dark cubbyhole to die. Eliza opened the door. The space wasn't a lot bigger than the area under her kitchen sink.

Marilyn almost smiled when she saw it. "This will do just fine—even has a lock, I see."

A lock? Things were looking up. You don't need a lock if you're dead.

"I think they plan to use it for hymnbooks, but they

haven't come yet." Obviously Baxter had seen no need to remove the old key from the lock when he painted the inside of the chapel.

"Okay, get inside—both of you!" Eliza felt a foot in her back. "They oughta find you eventually, but this should give us a start. Just remember, I have the baby. You'll be hearing from us about the ransom."

Eliza felt the older woman stumbling in behind her, and bit her lip to keep from crying out when a sharp heel dug into her instep. She landed on her hands and knees on the dusty floor and listened to the grating of the key being turned in the lock. The place was hot and stifling and smelled of mice, but she was relieved to be here. Something trailed across her neck, and Eliza shivered. A spider web?

"Olivia," Eliza said when the footsteps died away. "You're wonderful! I take back every rotten, nasty thing I ever said to you. What did you really do with Mattie?"

"Made a quick trade with a friend of mine," Olivia said. "She's safe and well with Julia Hershman in Sandy Springs. It was on the way." Olivia sneezed in the dark; Eliza felt her curl on the floor beside her, and for the first time was glad for her stepmother's diminutive size. "How long do you think it will take Marilyn to find out her 'captive' is a doll?" Olivia asked.

"About five minutes; maybe ten if we're lucky. She'll probably leave the 'baby' where she is until she moves my car out of sight. I hate to think what she'll do when she learns we tricked her."

Olivia sighed. "That big doll belongs to Julia's granddaughter. She's going to be most upset if she doesn't get it back."

Eliza giggled. For some reason, she found that extremely funny. "Wish I'd thought to go to the bathroom," she said.

"If I'd known I might die, I would've smoked one last cigarette," Olivia said. "Look, if I move my foot to the left, do you think you might readjust your elbow?"

Eliza obligingly complied. "You would've done what?"

"Smoked a cigarette. I'd just about kill for one right now."

"I didn't even know you smoked."

"Gave them up when I married your father. We made a bargain. He had to change his diet, and I stopped smoking the evil weed."

So that was why Olivia was so antsy! "I never even guessed."

"There are a lot of things you don't know."

Eliza brought her knees up to her chin. Her neck had a cramp in it. "Like?"

"Like how your daddy worries about you, loves you."

Eliza shrugged the clinging spider web away. "You don't understand," she said. "He's never approved of anybody I dated. There was a boy—well, a man—when I was younger. I saw him off and on for several years, and we planned to go away together. That was when Daddy told me that if I left with Chris Wylie, not to bother to come back home."

"So, you gave him up nobly. Did you love him?"

"Well . . . I guess I thought I did. And then there's Spencer. Daddy can't stand him either. He'd be perfectly happy if I settled down with some boring accountant and crocheted doilies for all the furniture."

"I happen to know Ben Figg has a fervent dislike of doilies," Olivia said. "But do you think that would've made a difference if you really felt strongly about either of these men?"

Eliza tried to find a place for her left arm. "That's what Sydney said."

"Spencer," Olivia said. "Just who is this Spencer? Tell me about him."

"Spencer G. Fillmore—an old friend, sort of. Met him in the Peace Corps."

"I thought that name sounded familiar. Dorcas said to tell you the florist delivered a huge arrangement of some kind of exotic lilies from him this afternoon. Said he'd be in touch soon."

"How does Dorcas know who sent them?"

"Read the card, of course."

"Nosy!" Eliza rubbed her nose. This should be interesting, she thought. Just when Charlie English comes along, up pops Spencer G. Fillmore. Well, he could just go back to Borneo—or wherever he came from! She didn't care if she ever saw him again. Eliza snorted under her breath.

She could sense Olivia stiffen beside her. "Damn it, Eliza, let's face it. This isn't about old boyfriends, is it? It's about me—and the fact that I married your father."

"Nothing personal, Olivia. It's just that you aren't my mother."

She laughed. "Can you ever forgive me for that?"

"I'm working on it," Eliza said, and sighed. Now her leg had a cramp in it. "I wish Daddy knew where we were!" Was that a footstep she heard outside?

"Never mind, your friend Kemper does . . . Damn! This door must be two inches thick." Olivia pounded it with dainty fists.

"You talked with Kemper?"

"Well, your neighbor Dorcas did. Nobody answered at Bellawood when I called from Julia's; you must've been downstairs. So I telephoned Dorcas to let somebody know I was on my way. She said Kemper had phoned there looking for you. They picked up Arnold Blodgett today at the gym."

Eliza wondered why Kemper hadn't called her at Bellawood, then remembered she had helped Genevieve with a tour for about an hour after she spoke with Olivia. It had helped to take her mind off her dilemma. She squirmed sideways. "So, where's Kemper now?"

"He was supposed to be on his way from Atlanta with some reporter. Said they planned to stop by Bellawood. Seems like they'd be here by now."

Eliza wished they would hurry. What if Marilyn came back first? "If they don't see our cars, they'll think we've gone . . . and they'll *never* find us in this closet! Maybe we can kick our way out. Ugh! What *is* that thing?" Eliza shifted to one side, shoving Olivia against the door.

"What thing?"

"Something keeps tickling my neck. Now it's trailing under my collar!" Could there be a snake in the closet with them? "What is it?"

Olivia fumbled around in the dark. "I feel like the blind man and the elephant, but I think it's a rope."

"A what?"

"A rope. Seems to be coming from the ceiling."

"The bell rope!" The two of them seized it together, and overhead the old copper bell began to wheeze, then clang. It had been cast long ago in England, when Pentecost Pitts ordered it for his new chapel.

Eliza had never heard the chapel bell ringing. They seldom used it, she was told, because of its harsh, annoying sound—like a giant throwing up, Baxter Phillips once said.

Eliza and Olivia Figg settled down to wait. You couldn't prove it by them.

M   Ballard, Mignon
                     Franklin.

                     Minerva cries
                     murder.

$18.95

DATE			
20x			